SECOND CHANCES IN HOLLYWOOD

Private Protection

Lauren —

Thank you for entering my giveaway! I hope you enjoy Alex & Miranda's story!

Mimi Francis

SECOND CHANCES IN HOLLYWOOD

MIMI FRANCIS

4 Horsemen
Publications, Inc.

4 Horsemen
Publications, Inc.

4 Horsemen Publications, Inc.
1497 Main St. Suite 169
Dunedin, FL 34698
4horsemenpublications.com
info@4horsemenpublications.com

Library of Congress Control Number: 2021944757

Paperback ISBN-13: 978-1-64450-350-8
Audiobook ISBN-13: 978-1-64450-348-5
Ebook ISBN-13: 978-1-64450-349-2

Dedication

This one is for my protector and my number one fan, my husband. You are my favorite person in the whole world. Thank you for believing in me and encouraging me to follow my dreams. I love you the mosterous!

Table of Contents

Chapter One

ALEX

Alex trudged past Primetime Security's receptionist and tried not to grimace at the young man. It wasn't his fault David summoned him to the office, insisting Alex come in immediately.

He wasn't used to being summoned; he mostly did his own thing and David let him, thanks to years of friendship. Sometimes he forgot he worked for Primetime Security until David called and demanded a favor. He'd reluctantly driven from his parents' place in rush hour traffic on his Saturday off to talk to his boss.

He was in Burbank for one reason and only one reason—his stupid sense of obligation. David needed a favor, and he knew Alex wouldn't say no.

He blew past David's assistant, opened the door to his boss's office, and stepped inside. David was on the phone, so Alex grabbed a bottle of water and sat on the sofa against the wall. He picked at a streak of paint on his jeans—he'd spent last weekend helping Chris and Sofia paint their house in the mountains before their wedding—and waited.

"Alex," David said as he hung up. "Thanks for coming up."

He took a sip of his water. "Why am I here, David?"

"Well, hello to you too," his boss scoffed.

Alex rolled his eyes. "Seriously, David, you dragged me up here because you need a favor. Tell me what it is so I can say 'no' and go home."

"Ha ha, you're funny."

"Talk."

David sighed. "Do you know who Miranda Putnam is?"

Alex squinted and downed his bottle of water. He wiped his mouth with the back of his hand. "No."

"She's an actress—"

"I don't work with actresses." He rolled his eyes. *I should've known this would be a waste of time.*

"At least hear me out," David said.

"Why?" Alex asked. "I've told you a million times, I don't work with actresses. They're full of themselves, bitchy, selfish, and dealing with them is impossible." He slammed the empty bottle down on the table; he shouldn't have to explain this, not after Courtney and Melissa. "Like I said, no." He rose to his feet. "I'll see you later."

David beat him to the door, blocking it with his body. "Okay, look, I *know* you don't like to work with actresses. Normally, I wouldn't ask, especially after what happened with Melis—" he cut himself off, his mouth snapping shut. He scrubbed a hand over his face and shook his head.

"David, stop. It's been almost two years for Christ's sake. I'm fine," he lied. "But that doesn't mean I'll work with an actress. I'll stick with actors, like Chris or my brother. No more actresses. I thought I made that clear."

"You did. Perfectly clear. But this is a special circumstance. Otherwise, I wouldn't ask. You know I wouldn't. Please sit down and listen to what I have to say," David begged. "You've got more experience than anyone on staff, and you're good with the complicated cases. All the stuff with Chris last spring proved that. This one is high profile, and I need someone I can trust." He held out a file. "Please?"

Alex grabbed the file with an irritated huff and moved back to the couch. "Why is it so high profile?" he asked.

David handed Alex another water, poured a drink for himself, and sat down. "She's an Oscar nominated actress, in the news more than she's not, philanthropist, humanitarian, drama queen, and colossal pain in the ass. And she's been receiving death threats. Death threats her latest studio is taking seriously. She's refused protection in the past, even fought against it, but she agreed this time for the next couple of weeks."

"Press junkets, charity events, photo shoots, and a movie premiere. She has a lot of public appearances scheduled," Alex said, flipping through the file. "Is one bodyguard going to be enough?"

"*You're* more than enough. You'll have to be enough. She's insisting there be only one bodyguard and a driver. You're my first and only choice for the job. I understand you don't want it; I do. But I am begging you. Please help me. It's for two weeks, three at the most. I tried to get Will down here from Vancouver, but his job doesn't end for another month, and I can't wait. If you do this for me, I will owe you big time."

"No shit." Alex shifted uneasily in his seat. "Why me? Why not call Rylan or even George? They're as qualified as I am. Hell, Rylan's better with the tech stuff, and George is itching to work with a big-name celebrity. Call one of them."

David leaned forward, elbows on his knees. "Your brother is in Vancouver with Will, and George isn't ready for something like this. Not yet, anyway. You're the man I want for the job. You came through the whole Chris Chandler debacle unscathed, not even a whisper of a word about Primetime Security in the press. You can handle this. I know you can. Come on, Alex. It's only for a few weeks. Please?"

Alex closed his eyes and pinched the bridge of his nose. If he was honest with himself, a two-to-three-week gig sounded right up his alley. With Chris living the domestic life in the mountains and Caleb not working for the last couple of months, he was between jobs. A quick, straightforward job was what he needed.

From what he saw in the file, this job would be easy. All he had to do was follow Miranda around to a few events and make sure she stayed safe. How complicated could it get? Guarding her would be easy, and it would satisfy the itch to do something. He had too much time to think, sitting around at his parents' house. A job would keep him occupied.

Besides, the overwhelming urge to protect was a constant presence in his life. Maybe it was because he was the oldest son, or his military service, or something deep inside him, but taking care of others, keeping them safe, made him happy. The need to protect was a part of his being. He felt it with his family, with his brothers, with Chris, and even Sofia. It was an addiction, a need he had to feed. Even after all the stuff with Melissa, the need was still there.

Glancing through the file on Miranda Putnam woke those protective feelings in him, and it would surely satisfy his need for excitement. Fighting it would be useless. No one deserved to feel helpless or frightened, not even a pain-in-the-ass actor. He rubbed the back of his neck and closed his eyes.

"When would I start?"

"Um, immediately. Like yesterday. Is that a yes?"

"It's a maybe," Alex corrected him. It was a yes, but not until his boss agreed to a few things. "There are a few stipulations I need you to agree to first. I need complete control, which means I get to pick the driver, and I get the discretion to bring on more staff—whether or not the princess likes it. Oh, and I want twice my normal fee."

"Twice? Are you joking?"

Alex shook his head and snorted. "Do you want me to take the job or not? If it's important to the studio, they'll pay it. Especially since I'm agreeing to do this on short notice. I'm supposed to go to Georgia with my brother next week, and if I take this job, I won't be able to go with Caleb. Oh, and I get Chris's wedding off. That is non-negotiable."

David was nodding before Alex even stopped talking. "Whatever you want. I'll get you the extra pay, you get Chris's wedding off, and I'll also let you pick who goes to Georgia with Caleb. Please, just tell me you'll do it."

"I'll do it." Alex pushed himself to his feet, the file in his hand. "Call the studio and her manager, get me her full itinerary. I'll start in the morning."

"Are you sure?" David asked with a sudden change of tone. "I know I was pushy, and after what you went through with Melissa—"

"Yes, I'm sure." Alex rolled his eyes. "It'll be fine." He yanked open the office door, not bothering to wait for David's reply. He was sick of convincing people he could do his job. It had been two years since everything with Melissa, and as far as anyone should be concerned, he had moved on. Miranda Putnam would help him prove it.

"Thank you!" David shouted after him.

"You're welcome," he called over his shoulder without turning around. He tucked the file under his arm and stalked back through the office. He needed a drink, probably more than one. The next couple of weeks would be interesting—he was sure of it.

Chapter Two

MIRANDA

"I agreed to it, Angela, but I'm not happy about it," Miranda bit out, letting the box of scripts fall onto the table inside the door. "I don't need a goddamn babysitter."

"I tried to talk the studio out of it, I swear," Angela said.

"Jesus, Miranda, we've gone over this a million times," Cooper interjected. "The letters were too personal. They're… they're crazy. Insane. Scary. The threats cannot be ignored, not anymore. Everybody knows you don't want protection, but we'll feel better if you accept this without being difficult."

Miranda sat on the couch in the small office and kicked off her shoes. She rubbed her forehead, attempting to stave off the creeping headache. She yanked a bottle of medicine from her purse and downed two pills with a glass of water from the end table.

I don't have time for a migraine. Not today. I have too much to do.

She ignored her brother and turned to her manager. Angela might listen to reason. "The bodyguard needs to stay out of my way, Ang." She resorted to her friend's pet name, a surefire way to get what she wanted. "These next three weeks are too important. With the movie premiere and the youth soccer center opening, I can't afford to be stifled."

"He will not stifle you, Mermaid—" Cooper said.

"They always stifle me," she interrupted. It didn't escape her attention that Cooper used the pet name tactic. The only people in her life who called her Mermaid were her brother and Angela. It was a twist on her name and a throwback to her first big role—a mermaid in a TV movie long forgotten. It launched her career, though.

Miranda pushed a hand through her hair, holding it away from her face, and closed her eyes. "They make all these demands, expect me to change my life around, follow their every direction, and act like gigantic Neanderthal assholes. I hate it."

"He won't stifle you; he'll protect you," Cooper said. "Right, Angela?"

Angela nodded. "It's only one bodyguard, the best Primetime Security has, shadowing you for the next two or three weeks. Once we sort this out, he's gone."

"Promise me you'll behave yourself and cooperate," Cooper added. "Be good and do as he asks."

"I promise." Miranda sighed, leaning back and resting her head on the back of the couch. "When does he start?"

"He'll be here first thing in the morning." Angela pulled her phone from her pocket and scrolled. "His name is Alex. Alex Peters."

"Sounds like a tool," Miranda mumbled, closing her eyes. "I can't wait."

Miranda made it through the day, no easy feat, considering the debilitating migraine she hadn't been able to hold off. There was too much going on for her to take time off work. Her days were busy, and today was no exception.

She and Cooper finalized the guest list for the fundraising dinner and hashed out the details for the ribbon-cutting ceremony at the soccer center. The Putnam Soccer Center was a joint effort between the two of them, a tribute to the parents they lost at a young age. Soccer was Cooper's passion, and Miranda was more than happy to support his efforts. They wanted to help others get involved in the sport that saved her brother's life and kept him out of trouble. With his uncanny soccer ability and her money, they created an amazing youth soccer facility for kids who couldn't afford to play the game. Cooper wanted everyone to experience the bliss he had playing his favorite game, and Miranda enjoyed paying it forward.

If that had been it for the day, it would have been enough, but she also did several phone interviews and went over a stack of scripts her agent gave her.

By the time she got away and headed upstairs to her room, her head throbbed like it was caught in a vise. The lights in her home office were too bright, and every noise was a nuclear bomb going off in her head. She closed the door, left the bedroom light off as she peeled off her clothes, and made her way to the bed. She crawled between the cool sheets and pulled the pillow over her head, muffling the sounds of the house. Tears leaked from the corner of her eyes as the pain overwhelmed her.

The migraines had started six weeks earlier. They scared her since she never suffered from them before. Her doctor chalked it up to stress, and everyone around her agreed. The new movie, the pressure to perform to her Academy-Award-nominee status, and the work she'd done to open the youth soccer center was only a small part of the intense stress she was under daily. It was no wonder she started suffering from migraines. Now she was lying in a dark room, unable to do anything because of a stupid headache. Unfortunately, the migraines forced her to change the way she did things, to make unnecessary adjustments, which only added to her stress.

Then there were the death threats. At first, Miranda hadn't taken them seriously. What celebrity hadn't gotten a few death threats? At least, that's what she told herself any time a new one appeared. They'd started as letters, then they'd graduated to emails and phone calls. She tried to act like they didn't bother her, but they terrified her. The last one, a text message sent to her private cell phone, had been the final straw. The studio insisted she hire a private security firm to protect her. She reluctantly agreed.

Miranda had hired bodyguards in the past for movie premieres or sometimes when she traveled, but she found them to be overbearing, demanding, and stifling. A bodyguard monitoring her every move killed any fun she wanted to have.

"Tolerate" was the only word to describe her acceptance of a bodyguard. She would tolerate him, but she wouldn't let him change her lifestyle or keep her from doing what she wanted.

The first thing she intended to do was remind her new bodyguard he worked for her. She was in charge, not him, and it would be crystal clear from the get-go. He would do what she said and follow her schedule. If he behaved himself, then maybe they could work together. If not, he would have to go.

Miranda dozed off, determined to set her new bodyguard straight the minute he arrived. He would know who was the boss before he made it through her front door.

Chapter Three

ALEX

A lex tugged on the collar of his shirt, wondering if he needed to get a bigger size. He hated suits, but the celebrities he protected expected him to look somewhat presentable, so he squeezed his 6'6", two-hundred-fifty-pound frame into one every time he worked. Today was no exception. He climbed into the black SUV, foregoing the seatbelt, and grunted at his new partner. Tiny pulled away from the curb and headed for Beverly Hills.

While they traveled through the shitty L.A. traffic, Alex once again flipped through Miranda's file. The techs at Primetime had done a background search on her, delving into her life to figure out who was targeting her. The information in her file went back to her childhood.

Miranda Putnam was thirty years old, a native Californian, and the oldest of two children. Her parents died in a car accident when she was ten and her sibling was three. She and her brother, Cooper, were raised by their grandparents. Miranda was a bright student with a fierce independent streak. She started acting in high school and continued through college, majoring in theatre arts before landing her first role in her early twenties. Since then, she'd been on an upward trajectory.

She seemed perfect, as did any celebrity, until you read between the lines. The press painted Ms. Putnam as a spoiled brat who ran away from her problems. According to her file, she went into hiding any time something didn't go her way. A broken engagement, lost movie roles, even not getting an award would send her off the grid. Miranda Putnam didn't like to talk about her problems or work through them. Running away was her modus operandi.

Four months ago, after she finished filming her newest movie, Miranda received her first death threat. It began with a few letters but escalated to emails and phone calls to her manager, the studio, and her home. The studio insisted she have twenty-four-hour private protection.

Miranda balked, claiming it wasn't serious; all popular actors got the occasional death threat. She wasn't wrong, but the threats against her grew more severe and frightening. It surprised him they'd waited so long to hire security. Someone should have done it much sooner.

Her dislike of bodyguards must have caused the delay. She refused them multiple times over the years, at times to her own detriment. She was stubborn, independent, and headstrong. Or in his words, a pain in the ass.

Alex closed the file as Tiny turned into the drive leading to Miranda's home. He eyed the grounds and the multiple entrance points along the waist-high fence. He scrubbed a hand over face and groaned. Tiny snorted beside him and pulled to a stop at the base of a set of stairs leading to the main doors of the enormous mansion.

"You thinking what I'm thinking?" Tiny asked.

"Yeah," Alex sighed. "This is gonna be a fucking nightmare." He stepped out of the SUV and straightened his jacket as he looked around the grounds. He was already on edge. No one manned the gate, and there wasn't a single person stationed outside the house. *Nightmare*.

He turned back to the SUV. "Tiny? Check the perimeter, will you? This is a clusterfuck, and it's not even seven a.m."

His partner chuckled as he climbed out of the SUV. "On it, boss," he said and took off around the house.

Tony "Tiny" Waltham was a good guy—dependable, smart, and intimidating at six feet tall and nearly three hundred pounds. Not as big as Alex, but he made for a daunting presence. He'd worked for Primetime Security since 2011. He was one of the best men on staff and by far the best driver. Alex had worked with him several times over the years; Tiny was an asset to any security team. Alex insisted David pull him off his current job and assign him to Miranda's team. David had readily agreed.

Alex trudged up the stairs and knocked on the front door, expecting a housekeeper or other household staff to answer. The door flew open, and he came face to face with Miranda Putnam.

Startled, he took a step back. The only pictures he'd seen of the actor were the few old photographs and the blurry copies of press releases in her file. The resemblance caught him off-guard; it was uncanny and, frankly, eerie. Miranda Putnam looked like a younger version of Melissa, with her turquoise blue eyes, her caramel brown hair, and her shapely figure. He wished David had told him the actor was a doppelganger of his wife. His *dead* wife.

It wasn't just the hair and the face; the bright light in her eyes and the way she carried herself—strong and confident with her shoulders back and a slight don't-mess-with-me smirk on her face—reminded him of Melissa.

Miranda Putnam was at least six feet tall—several inches taller than Melissa—with gorgeous curves that men probably fought to get their hands on, brilliant, unusual turquoise blue eyes, and carefully coiffed, caramel brown hair with subtle blonde highlights. She had full pink lips, now turned down in an irritated frown. She crossed her arms over her perfect breasts and stared at him.

Alex swallowed back the lump rising in his throat. "Ms. Putnam?"

"You must be Alex Peters," she said, bending over to fix the strap on one of her heels, giving him quite the view of those perfect breasts. He closed his eyes and prayed for strength.

"You're right on time, thank God," she continued. "And it's Miranda. Ms. Putnam was my mother and grandmother." She finished fixing her shoe, pushed past him, and hurried toward the SUV.

So that was how this was going to go. He needed to nip the attitude in the bud. Alex followed her, grabbed her upper arm, and yanked her to a stop before she hit the bottom of the stairs. She turned, a deadly glare on her face. She tried to pull her arm away, but he held tight. Her mouth opened, most likely to protest, but he cut her off before she could say anything.

"Let's get a few things straight, *Ms. Putnam*," he growled. "I'm here to keep you safe. For me to do that, you are going to listen to me whether or not you like it."

She exhaled sharply and rolled her eyes. "Look, Mr. Peters, I only agreed to a bodyguard because the studio insisted on it." She tapped the center of his chest with a manicured finger. "You want to make both of our lives easy? You listen to me, go where I say when I say, and above all else, stay the hell out of my way." She spun around, stumbling in her high heels when Alex didn't release her.

Alex had known this job would be difficult, but protecting someone with an attitude who didn't want him anywhere near her made it damn near impossible. It took less than five minutes with the temperamental actress for him to regret taking this job.

Tiny emerged from the side of the house, nodded at Alex, and headed for the SUV. Alex released Miranda's arm and gestured for her to go ahead of him. She gave him a dirty look before stomping away.

"We'll see about that, ma'am," he mumbled under his breath.

Chapter Four

MIRANDA

Miranda didn't know what to expect when she opened her front door, but it certainly wasn't the giant, tanned, dark-haired, body-to-die for Adonis in a suit. The few times she had a bodyguard, they'd been scary, tattooed guys with arms bulging out of tight t-shirts, cargo pants straining to contain their over-muscled thighs, and flat-top haircuts. Alex Peters seemed cool and confident. And good God, the man was perfectly muscled in all the right places. His blue suit fit him like a glove and made his light blue eyes sparkle. He had short hair, shaved on the side and longer on the top, slightly tousled like he'd been running his fingers through it. Through his neatly trimmed beard, he had a perpetual smirk on his face. He was the most attractive men she'd ever seen, and she worked with the most handsome men in the world.

The man's deep, whiskey-thick voice sent chills down her spine and made her brain fizzle out. She was a sucker for a nice body and a delicious voice, which Alex Peters had in spades. She wasn't dating anyone; maybe a quick fling with her bodyguard would do her good. She wouldn't be the first actor to indulge.

Too bad he was a cold, standoffish jerk. He sat beside her in the backseat of the predictable black SUV, staring straight ahead, his smooth voice washing over her as he explained how he did things. Miranda could have melted listening to him talk if she wasn't fuming over the orders he tossed around. Her hands clenched at her sides, her nails digging into her palms as he listed all the things she would have to change: mixing up her daily routine, hiring security for the mansion, vetting all of her hired help, having an escort everywhere she went, and even changing which stores she normally shopped. In the blink of an eye, her freedom disappeared all because of some meaningless death threats. It was exactly why she didn't want a bodyguard.

The SUV pulled to a stop in front of the Beverly Hills Hotel where the press junket was being held. Miranda went for the door, but Alex reached past her and held it closed. She ground her teeth together and tried not to scream.

"I'll come around and open the door. Stay put." Alex disappeared out the other side of the car.

Miranda rolled her eyes and let out a muted scream of frustration. She caught the driver's eyes in the rear-view mirror. "Is he always this annoying?" she asked.

The man's eyes narrowed, and he snorted. "Only when he's trying to keep someone from getting killed." He stepped out of the car and slammed the door behind him.

She rubbed her forehead and prayed the twitching behind her eye didn't mean another headache. She knew she was being a bitch and showcasing every stereotype about snotty, spoiled actresses in existence. Shit, every stereotype people believed about her. These men were trying to keep her safe, not ruin her life. She should try to be more cooperative. It would make the studio and Cooper happy. Her brother had already given her one lecture about playing nice, and she didn't need another.

The door beside her opened, and Alex appeared, his hand out. She took it and let him help her from the vehicle, giving him a smile she hoped would smooth over her bitchiness. Alex glanced at her, his back ramrod straight, his hands balled into tight fists at his side, and his face hard and stoic. It scared her a little.

Miranda gritted her teeth. She deserved it for being unreasonable and difficult. She swallowed her pride and smiled wider.

"Sorry for being a pain," she said. "I'm not a fan of bodyguards."

"So I've heard," he growled.

The sound sent a tingle dancing down her spine. *Jesus, that voice.*

"Don't believe everything you've heard. I'm not that bad." She tried another smile. *Why am I trying so hard?*

Alex grunted incoherently and rolled his eyes.

So much for trying to be nice. "Do you ever smile?" she demanded.

Alex stared at her, no expression on his face.

"Guess not." She spun on her heel and stomped across the cement courtyard to the building. Behind her, Alex sighed loudly and followed.

Angela waited in the lobby and rushed over as soon as she saw Miranda, smiling and nodding at Alex before taking Miranda's arm and leading her deep into the hotel. As they walked, Angela filled her in on the schedule. Miranda's head pounded. It was going to be a long day.

In the elevator, Alex stood in front of the doors with his broad back to her and his arms crossed, making his biceps bulge. His intimidating, off-putting stance would keep everyone away from her.

Angie took her arm and dragged her to the back of the elevator. "Your bodyguard is attractive," she whispered in Miranda's ear.

Miranda shook her head, a forced smile plastered on her face. She shouldn't be surprised Angie found Alex attractive. She'd loved good-looking men since college and tended to get herself in trouble because of them. Back in college—when both of them struggled to find acting jobs—a late night with a guy she'd picked up in a bar cost Angie a part in a movie after a bad audition. Thanks to him, she'd stayed up late drinking, shown up late with a hangover, and bombed it. Coincidentally, it was the same mermaid movie that catapulted Miranda into the spotlight. Angie liked to joke how if she'd gotten the part, their roles would be reversed—Angie, the actress, and Miranda, the manager.

If Miranda didn't watch out, Angie would steal her bodyguard away for a private one-on-one time. It wouldn't be the first time Angela snaked a man away from Miranda. She would have to watch Alex and Angela. The thought of them together made her skin crawl.

The elevator doors opened, and Alex stepped out, peered up and down the corridor, then gestured for Miranda and Angela to come out. Angela blew past him, winking as she brushed up against him.

"Follow me," she said in a sing-song voice.

Alex walked beside Miranda, his hand a comforting weight on the small of her back. His cologne—something spicy mixed with sage and leather—washed over her and made her long to bury her face against his chest and breathe him in. She gnawed on the inside of her cheek, reminding herself this man worked for her and was there to protect her. She couldn't fall for him, no matter how attractive she found him.

They stopped outside one of the conference rooms. Alex opened the door and ducked inside alone. He returned a few seconds later, tipping his chin once in her direction.

"Looks good," he said before settling into a seat outside the door, one foot propped on his knee, his jacket unbuttoned. The seams on his pants looked ready to give any second.

Jesus, Miranda, stop ogling your damn bodyguard.

"Um, what are you doing?" Angela asked.

"I'm waiting right here," Alex explained. He spoke to her like she was a child.

Angela's eyes narrowed. "Why don't you wait downstairs in the car?"

Miranda put a hand on Angela's elbow. "It's okay, Angie. He can wait there. A bodyguard can't guard my body from ten floors away."

Angie gave her a weird look, but Miranda ignored it. She stepped into the conference room and took a seat in one of the plush chairs, her manager right behind her. Angela knew better than to question her. Besides, what else would she say? *I'm cooperating because he's hot?* She would *not* tell Angela she found her bodyguard attractive. She would take that one to her grave.

"Let's get this thing started, shall we?" Miranda deflected.

Angela nodded and handed her an open bottle of water. Miranda took a sip, wincing when the cold water sent a shooting pain through the center of her head. At least, she hoped it was because of the water.

As the door opened and the first reporter came in, Miranda glimpsed Alex sitting outside. It made her feel better knowing he was there.

Not gonna tell him that, though.

Chapter Five

ALEX

Alex stifled a yawn and checked his watch for the hundredth time. According to Angela, Miranda's flirty manager, the press junket should wrap up within the hour. Then it was back to her mansion for a few hours before a party at a studio executive's house in the Hills.

He wanted this day to be over. Miranda and her uncanny resemblance to Melissa had rattled him. Her attitude had rattled him even more because he liked it and he liked *her*, something he couldn't wrap his head around. He wasn't sure if it was because she was gorgeous or because she reminded him of his wife. He pinched the bridge of his nose and silently chastised himself.

I shouldn't be sitting here thinking how gorgeous my client is.

Restless, he paced back and forth in front of the large bank of windows, sipping a cup of watered-down coffee from the craft services room. He'd run into a few familiar faces—other bodyguards and security personnel he met working events with Chris or Caleb. One of them was a former employee of Primetime Security, Brady Gaither. He considered saying hello—they'd parted on not-so-stellar terms—but Gaither disappeared into the crowd before Alex could approach him.

"Alex?" Angela tapped him on the shoulder. "Miranda's ready to go. We need to make it quick, too. She's not feeling well."

"Is she okay?" he asked.

"She's fine. It's just a headache. She needs to rest, and then she'll be as good as new. She should be here in a minute. Take her straight home. Tell her I'll be over later."

Angela squeezed his forearm before hurrying down the hall to the elevator. She waved at him with a smile and a wink as the door slipped closed. She was too flirty; avoiding her was probably a good idea.

Five minutes later, Miranda came out the door, face pinched and her arms crossed. She didn't look "fine" to him. In fact, she looked awful. She didn't pause. Instead, she marched past him and headed for the elevator. Alex hurried to catch up with her and slipped in before the doors closed.

Alex maneuvered the two of them to the back of the crowded elevator, his hand on her hip, his body between her and everyone else inside. She looked up at him, her turquoise blue eyes brimming with tears.

"Are you alright?" he asked.

"Not really. Migraine. I get them a lot. I…I just want to go home and sleep."

The urge to wrap his arms around this woman and hold her close came over him. She seemed so vulnerable—nothing like the sassy, strong-minded woman he met this morning.

"Let's get you home," he whispered.

Miranda nodded and leaned against the elevator wall, her eyes closed.

Alex waited for the elevator to empty before he led her through the immense crowd in the lobby. Through the glass windows, he saw Tiny beside the SUV, sunglasses on, scanning the crowd. Alex raised a hand to get his attention. Tiny straightened and grabbed the car door, ready to open it.

Someone yelled Miranda's name as they stepped outside. In seconds, her name was being called from all directions. She turned toward the crowd, but Alex kept his hand in the center of her back, guiding her toward the car, looking for a gap or break he could push through. Someone jostled his elbow. He turned, and the next thing he knew, Miranda was gone.

"Miranda!" Alex yelled. He swung around, but he didn't see her. He held a finger to his ear, activating his earpiece. "Tiny?"

"I'm right here." His partner appeared at his side. "Where is she?"

"I don't know. She was right next to me, and I was walking her to the car, then she disappeared. We need to find her. Now."

They separated, pushing through the crowd of people, calling Miranda's name, ignoring the dirty looks from the surrounding people. Out of the corner of his eye, Alex thought he saw a brunette head turned his way and someone calling his name. He darted between two cyclists and around the fountain in front of the building.

"Miranda!"

The brunette turned, her pain-filled, turquoise eyes locking on his, and the group of people surrounding her spun in unison to look at him. Alex ignored them, irritated but used to obnoxious crowds of fans. His only concern was Miranda. As he moved through the crowd, he heard a loud pop behind him, and a chunk of concrete near Miranda's foot exploded.

"Miranda!"

A scream echoed off the skyscrapers above their heads, and the crowd surged, trying to get away from whatever had caused the concrete to explode. Alex pushed past the running people and leaped in front of Miranda. He wrapped his arms around her and tried to shove her toward the SUV. The crowd moved as one entity, intent on getting away from the famous actress standing in their midst when moments ago they'd been surrounding her, harassing her. He and Miranda were bumped and jostled from all sides.

Tiny shouted Alex's name, prompting Alex to move toward the sound of his partner's voice. But his feet tangled with Miranda's, and they fell to the ground. He shifted in the air, and his body landed lightly on hers, shielding her from danger. His only concern was to protect her.

Tiny pushed through the crowd, shoving people out of the way. Alex scooped Miranda up while Tiny cleared a path to the SUV, using his body to block the surging crowd. He held her close as they sprinted for the car.

But before Alex could open the door, there was another pop, and a hole appeared in the Escalade's side.

Alex stumbled back a step, dragging Miranda with him. "What the fuck?"

"Alex, move!" Tiny shouted.

Alex twisted to his right and reached for the door handle. A sharp sting hit his arm, and pain exploded through the bicep. Tiny emerged from the crowd and ripped open the back door. Alex shoved Miranda inside and stumbled in after her, cursing under his breath. Tiny appeared in the driver's seat and threw the car in gear, the tires squealing as he tore away from the curb.

"Ow. Fuck," Miranda moaned, pushing Alex off of her as she struggled to sit up, her hand to her head. "If I didn't know any better, I'd think *you* were trying to kill me."

She pulled her hand away from her head, and her eyes widened at the red covering her fingers. "Is that… is that blood?"

"No, Miranda," Alex breathed out. "It's okay." He cupped her chin and turned her head. It *was* blood, but it was probably from the wound on his arm. He had sprawled all over her after they fell into the SUV.

She stared at him, tears in the corner of her eyes, her face pale and frightened. "I don't feel so good, Alex," she said right before she fainted.

Chapter Six

ALEX

"You idiot!" David yelled.

Alex held the phone away from his ear, wincing as his boss screamed in his ear. Nothing David said could be as bad as what Alex had told himself.

"I know—"

"Shut up," David growled. "I trusted you to handle this, Alex. First day on the job, and you get her shot?"

"She didn't get shot," Alex snapped, pacing back and forth in the small space beside the hospital bed. "She hit her head on the concrete and had to get a couple of stitches. I'm the one who got shot."

"What the fuck happened, Alex? Tell me everything."

"It was her fans. If you can call them that. Someone spotted her, shouted her name, and the next thing I knew, we were separated. Then, out of nowhere, someone shot at her. I jumped in front of her, but on the way to the car, our feet tangled and we fell. She hit her head when we went down, and somewhere along the way, I caught a bullet in the arm. Tiny drove us straight to the hospital."

"Jesus, the death threats have escalated to attempts on her life." David cursed.

"I don't know, boss; it was weird. Whoever it was should have hit her, but they didn't," Alex said. "I think they missed on purpose."

"Maybe trying to scare her?"

"That's my guess. If they wanted her dead, she would be. I think it was an opportunity to scare her. Tiny's back at the hotel, working with the police and trying to dig up information."

"Okay," David said. He exhaled loudly. "I'm sorry. I know you did your best. Working with celebrities is always unpredictable. Are you okay?"

"I'm fine. Bullet grazed my arm. The doctor bandaged it a few minutes ago. I'm waiting to be released so I can check on Ms. Putnam."

"I'm glad you're okay," David said. "Keep me posted. And I expect an update in the morning from you and Tiny. First thing."

"Will do, boss. I'll call you later." He disconnected the call and shoved his phone in his pocket. His chest was tight, and he couldn't catch his breath. Alex bent over, his hands on his knees, and squeezed his eyes shut.

The sound of the gunshots echoed in his head, an accusation and a reminder of a past he struggled to forget. Red obscured his vision.

It's not the same as Melissa. It's fine. Everything is fine.

The doctor pulled the curtain of the tiny room back, startling him. He bolted upright, his head spinning. He grabbed the edge of the bed to keep himself upright. The ER doctor who bandaged his arm stood in front of him.

"Are you okay, Mr. Peters?"

"Yeah, I'm fine. A little woozy, maybe. I'm good enough to go home." He perched on the edge of the bed and crossed his arms, wincing as the wound on his bicep protested.

Alex spent a few minutes talking to the doctor before signing his aftercare information. He shoved the paperwork in his jacket pocket and asked to see Ms. Putnam.

A nurse led him through a maze of rooms to a secluded corner room away from the other patients. He'd insisted on privacy, and they had been more than happy to oblige. The hospital had seen its fair share of celebrities over the years; they knew how to handle it.

The nurse pulled open a glass door covered by a curtain. Miranda sat on the bed, staring at the wall, arms crossed, a small bandage on her temple. She gave Alex a dirty look.

"Hey, how are you feeling?"

"Like shit," she scoffed. "I want to go home."

"I'll get her discharge paperwork," the nurse said. "Give me a few minutes."

Alex nodded, pulled out his phone, and sent a text to Tiny, instructing him to find a place away from the press to pick them up. He finished typing and leaned against the wall by the door, intent on staying as far from Miranda as possible. She wasn't happy to see him.

Miranda glared at the wall, and Alex stared at the floor for a few tense and uncomfortable minutes. He couldn't look at her; he kept picturing her passed out in the SUV, limp and pale, blood covering her face.

It scared the shit out of him, reminding him of Melissa lying on the floor, limp, pale, and bloody— dying. He thought the wounds were healed. He was wrong.

Miranda sighed loudly, an obvious attempt to get his attention. "I need to get out of here."

"It shouldn't be much longer," Alex said.

"I fucking hate hospitals," she muttered. "I want to go home."

Alex didn't respond—not that he wanted to— because his phone rang, earning him an irritated huff from the put-upon actress.

"Peters."

It was Tiny. "Hey boss, I found a place out of sight, but it'll take me a few minutes to get there." He told Alex where to meet him.

"Perfect. I'll see you in a bit," Alex said.

He cut the call short when the nurse returned. It only took a few minutes to get the discharge paper-work signed and Miranda in the wheelchair. She grumbled but agreed to follow hospital rules.

The nurse led them through the hallways to a door leading out to a dark alley. Alex thanked her and promised they wouldn't move until their car arrived. She reluctantly left them to wait. He leaned against the door, staring out the window, his back to Miranda.

After a few minutes, she cleared her throat. "I'm sorry about what I said earlier." Her voice was so low he almost missed it.

"Excuse me?" He turned toward her, his eyes locking on her brilliant blue ones.

"When I said you were trying to kill me? I didn't mean it. And…" She exhaled, drawing it out for a few seconds. "I'm also sorry for being difficult and bitchy. You're trying to do your job, to protect me. I…I shouldn't argue with you. I'll try to do whatever you need me to. You tell me, I'll do it."

"Really?" Alex scoffed. "You don't seem too thrilled—"

"That was before someone took a shot at me," she snapped before her mouth closed, her teeth clicking together. She sucked in a deep breath. "I'm sorry. Yes, I'm sure. Whatever I have to do."

Alex smiled. "Thank you. I appreciate the cooperation. And I promise you that we will sort this out."

Miranda gave him a weary smile, and damn if it didn't make his heart try to pound out of his chest. He longed to touch her, push the hair away from her face, caress the wound on her head, and take away her pain. Every second he spent with her messed with his head. It was as if the woman he loved was still alive. He pinched the bridge of his nose and stared out the window.

"I guess I missed the party at the exec's house," she grumbled, dragging his attention back to her.

"Your manager was going to go and smooth things over," Alex reassured her.

Miranda shook her head. "It doesn't matter what she says. I'll be fodder for the press. 'Miranda Putnam misses yet another important event.' Blah, blah, blah."

"I'm sure it will be fine." He kept his eyes glued to a spot above her head, childishly refusing to make eye contact.

Miranda fidgeted with her phone, turning it over in her hands again and again. She jumped when it vibrated and squinted as she opened it to read the text.

Alex turned back to the window, praying Tiny would show up with the SUV soon. He wanted to get Miranda home so she could rest; her furrowed, pinched brow and pale face made him uneasy. Plus, he needed a drink and a chance to clear his head.

"Alex?" Miranda whispered.

"Hm?" he hummed, continuing to stare out the door.

"Alex!"

"What?" He turned to face her.

She held her phone out with a trembling hand. He couldn't make out what was on the screen, so he snatched it, saving it from hitting the floor as it shook out of her hand.

I told you what would happen if you left the house. Next time, I won't miss.

Chapter Seven

MIRANDA

A good night's sleep was all she needed to pull herself together. *Maybe if I say it enough, I'll believe it.* She was a shaking, crying mess when Alex helped her into the car and had escalated into a full-on panic attack by the time they got back to her house. Her entire body shook, she was nauseous, and everything seemed to spin.

Miranda refused to let Alex leave until she called her assistant and best friend, Tara. Alex's assurances that Primetime Security's best men were stationed outside had done nothing to ease her worries. She would feel better with her friend here.

best friend swooped in and sprinted through the kitchen door like her ass was on fire, pink and blue hair flying out of its braid, wearing one of her ridiculous t-shirts with a cow on it saying "Moo, Bitch." She pounced on Miranda the second she saw her, hugging her so hard she couldn't breathe. Despite the lack of oxygen, Tara's arrival had a calming effect on her.

"Oh my God, I've been so worried about you," Tara squeaked, her eyes brimming with tears. "When I saw the news—"

"Shit! It's on the news?" Miranda rolled her eyes and sighed.

Tara nodded and handed her a tablet. Every news and gossip site on the web had posted about what happened, most of it wildly inaccurate. Speculation gone crazy. The Gossip Monger, the worst of the worst, claimed she was lying in the hospital, near death after a disgruntled fan took a shot at her.

Furious and ready to blow, Miranda swore she would call every goddamn news—and fake news—outlet herself and tell them to get their fucking stories straight.

"Okay, knock it off," Tara snapped.

"Knock what off?" Miranda asked innocently.

"I know what you're thinking. Let it go. It won't matter what you say to the press. They'll say what they want, whether or not it's the truth."

Miranda nodded, wincing when the movement made her head throb. A head wound on top of the usual headache made her feel as if she were floating outside her body, the pain too unbearable to deal with on a normal, human level.

"You need to get some rest," Tara said. "Let's get you to bed."

"I think that's a great idea," a gruff voice said from the other side of the room.

Miranda had forgot Alex was in the corner of the kitchen, hovering like an annoying gnat. She squeezed her eyes closed and reminded herself she was the one who insisted he stay with her until Tara arrived. She asked him to be annoying.

"You're both right," Miranda mumbled. "I need sleep." She pushed herself away from the kitchen table and wobbled to her feet.

Alex swooped in, his arm slipping around her waist. He helped her upstairs and deposited her in her room. Tara followed behind then ushered Alex out the door, closing it firmly behind him. She waited about two point six seconds.

"Christ on a cracker, that man is hot," she whispered. "He exudes masculinity, doesn't he? How the hell did you sit in a car with him without jumping on him?"

Miranda shrugged. "Well, the head wound helped."

"Ha ha, you're funny. I'm serious—he's freaking hot. Is he single?"

"I don't know. The subject never came up." Miranda peeled off her blood-stained clothes, leaving them in a pile on the floor, and contemplated taking a shower. Sleep seemed the better option. She pulled on the t-shirt and shorts she'd left on the end of the bed and crawled between the sheets.

"I wanna sleep," she mumbled.

"Fine. We'll talk about your gorgeous bodyguard in the morning."

The morning light found Miranda headache-free, relaxed, and more together than she had been in a while. Her hands no longer shook, and her stomach was calm enough to eat. After a good night's sleep, she realized she'd been melodramatic yesterday. Someone was trying to scare her, not kill her. If they wanted her dead, she would be. Period. Life could go on as normal.

After a warm shower, she was almost human again. She dressed in jeans and a sweatshirt and went looking for Tara, finding her in the kitchen with her tablet and a fresh pot of coffee brewing on the counter.

"Morning, Tara," she said, smiling.

"Hey!" Tara dropped the tablet, hurried across the room, and took Miranda's arm, looking into her eyes. "How are you?"

"I'm fine," she muttered, pulling away, and went to grab a coffee mug from the cupboard. She was sick of people making a fuss over her. Last night, she let her guard down, opened herself up, and let herself be vulnerable. But it was a new day, and she wanted everyone to act as if things were normal, which meant no more hovering or babying the actress.

"What's on my agenda today?" Miranda asked, pouring herself a cup of coffee.

Tara rolled her eyes, but she grabbed her tablet and gave Miranda a quick rundown of her day, culminating in the fundraiser for the youth soccer center later in the evening. A five-hundred-dollar-a-plate fundraiser she would not miss, not when she was spearheading the event.

"Is Cooper here?" she asked.

Tara shook her head. "No, he said he had an early practice and a meeting. He wouldn't say with who but said to tell you he would see you tonight."

"Of course, he did." Her younger brother was unpredictable. It drove her mad. She checked the clock on the wall. It was almost nine a.m. She was running behind.

"Have you seen my bodyguard?"

"Your bodyguard?" Tara smirked. "The muscle-bound, blue-eyed, brooding guy with the deep voice? That bodyguard?"

"Yeah, the so-attractive-you-want-to-die bodyguard," Miranda said with a grin. "His name is Alex, by the way. Have you seen him?"

"Yep. He's dreamy." Tara sighed.

"And you're not fifteen." Miranda laughed. "Have you seen him *recently*? As in, do you know where he is?"

"He's in the office under the stairs, the one with all the broken monitors."

Miranda nodded and hurried back through the mansion to the security office, a room no one ever used. Shortly after she moved in, she had all the cameras disconnected. The thought of having every move she made recorded gave her the creeps.

Alex hung up his phone when she stepped into the office. He shoved it into his pocket, a grim look on his face. He pointed to the blank monitors.

"None of these work?" he asked.

"Good morning to you, too," she said. "And no, they don't work. I had them disconnected. Why?"

"Well, they're being reconnected today. David is sending over a crew," Alex explained. "We'll reconnect them and upgrade any outdated equipment."

"I don't want them—"

Alex gave her a look that silenced her. "No arguments."

"Bullshit," Miranda snapped. "This is my house, my life. I don't want it under scrutiny. Those cameras will not be reconnected. I refuse to be under twenty-four-hour surveillance in my own home."

"Do you want to be dead?" he growled.

"No one is trying to kill me! This is all stupid."

"It is not stupid. Someone shot at you. They threatened your life via text message to your *private* cell phone. I take it seriously even if you don't. If I can't keep you locked down, I will do what I can to protect you."

"This is so ridiculous," she huffed.

"Goddamn it, Melissa, why can't you let me protect you?"

Alex froze, his eyes wide, his fists clenched at his sides. He cleared his throat, stared over her shoulder, and refused to make eye contact with Miranda.

"Melissa?" she asked. "Who's Melissa?"

"It's not important."

Miranda didn't believe it for one second. She opened her mouth to ask again, but he cut her off.

"I'm not arguing with you. The cameras are being reinstalled." He pushed past her and marched toward the front door. "I'm going to check in with Tiny. I need your itinerary for the day." He turned back to her. "Unless I can convince you to stay home."

She shook her head. "Sorry."

"Figures." Alex scoffed. "Get me your itinerary, so I know what I'm up against."

Miranda knew what he was up against—her stubborn ass refusing his help. She needed to get over it and let him protect her. Accepting any help was difficult for her; she had always taken care of herself and her little brother. Relying on someone went against every fiber of her being. Maybe she didn't take the death threats seriously, but everyone around her did.

She pushed a hand through her hair and followed him into the foyer. *Stop being a diva, Miranda.* All she had to do was play nice for two weeks, suck it up, and let him protect her without acting like her life was over.

"Alex?"

He stopped, though he didn't turn, his shoulders tense. "Yeah?"

"Do you own a tux?"

Chapter Eight

ALEX

He hated tuxedos. Hated them. Wearing a regular suit wasn't much better, but tuxedos really annoyed him. He tugged on the collar, hoping it might help make him more comfortable. It didn't.

When Miranda told him why he needed a tux, Alex considered getting someone to cover for him, but he didn't want to push his luck. She was being cooperative, and he didn't dare jinx it. He could have stayed outside with the other bodyguards, but Miranda made it clear she wanted him inside like any other guest. It was the only way she would agree to his presence.

He avoided being alone with her all day; he was too fucked in the head. The similarities between her and Melissa were too much. He found himself attracted to her, but he didn't know if it was because she was beautiful or because she reminded him of the woman he'd loved and lost. Calling her "Melissa" had messed with him. So, he escaped and found things to keep himself busy—talking to Tiny, directing the reinstallation of the cameras, going over her itinerary with a fine-tooth comb—anything to avoid her.

But now, it was only him, charged with her protection and watching her every move. It would have been torture if she wasn't so damn gorgeous.

Alex tracked Miranda as she mingled and chatted with everyone in the room, smiling and laughing, while her brother, Cooper, trailed behind her. Now and then, she'd touch the bandage on her head and the bruise blossoming beneath it, shrugging and waving off any comments about it. She was obviously in her element.

She was breathtaking in a long, off-the-shoulder, purple gown, her curled hair skimming her shoulders and her beautiful blue eyes shining. Everything about her was stunning: the way she moved, the way she carried herself, her smile, her laugh. Everything.

Alex rubbed a hand over his face and pinched the bridge of his nose. He needed to snap out of it and stop lusting after his client.

"Well, shit, if it isn't Alex Peters." The voice came from behind him—loud, obnoxious, and familiar. He turned, praying it wasn't who he thought it was, and sighed.

Brady Gaither.

David hired Alex and Gaither at the same time. Two years ago, shortly before Melissa's death, David let Gaither go after several high-level clients complained about his behavior. David asked Alex to dig into the complaints, and he discovered Gaither made aggressive, unwanted advances toward their female clients, lied about his duties to get more money, dumped important jobs on untrained subordinates, and committed a multitude of other offenses. David confronted Gaither, showed him the evidence Alex uncovered, and fired him. Gaither was angrier than Alex had ever saw him, threatening to pay them back for destroying his life. No one had seen him since, though Alex heard through the grapevine that he was working as an independent security consultant.

"Brady, how you been?" Alex asked, shaking Gaither's hand. There was no way this conversation would go well.

"I'm good." Gaither smiled, pumping Alex's arm furiously, an odd look on his face. "Dude, I was so sorry to hear about Melissa. That sucks. How you holding up?"

"I'm okay." He shrugged. He was wary of Gaither's pleasant attitude, but if he was going to be friendly, Alex would be too. "You here on a job?"

"Yep. Some pompous ass forking over a shit ton of money to the charity, trying to get in the lady of the hour's pants." Gaither laughed. "You?"

Alex pointed at Miranda. "The lady of the hour."

"Holy hell. She's a hot commodity. How do you always get the attractive clients?" Gaither tipped his head to the side, scrutinizing Miranda. "Wow, she looks like Melissa, doesn't she?"

Alex bristled. He gritted his teeth and said, "A little, I guess."

Gaither elbowed him in the side. "From what I hear, you've got your work cut out for you. Word has it she's a pistol."

"She is definitely a handful." Alex laughed.

"Oh, really?" Gaither chuckled and winked. "You should fill me in on the details."

Miranda caught his eye and gestured for him to join her. Alex adjusted his jacket and tie. "Excuse me, but I need to go. Have a good night."

"Let's grab a beer and catch up sometime!" Gaither called after him.

Alex didn't acknowledge Gaither, silently praying it wouldn't happen. He hurried to Miranda's side. She was pale with deep, purple circles under her eyes. He took her elbow and let her lean against him.

"You okay?" he whispered, his mouth pressed to her ear. Her fresh scent filled his nostrils.

"I'm tired." She smiled tightly, her brow furrowed and her eyes half open, filled with pain. "I have a terrible headache. Do you think you can get me out of here without making an issue out of it?"

"Absolutely," he said, glancing at the nearest exit. "I'll have Tiny pick us up at the side entrance."

"Give me one minute." She made her way across the room, grabbed Cooper, and pulled him aside, whispering. He nodded and kissed her cheek before vanishing into the crowd. She watched him for a minute then returned to Alex's side.

"Cooper is going to cover for me," she explained. "Let's get out of here."

Forty-five minutes later, they drove past the mansion gate and up the drive. Miranda was unusually quiet; she didn't stir until Tiny parked in the shadows next to the house.

Alex opened the door, helped Miranda from the car, and followed her into the house. He watched her as she slipped off her heels, tossed them on an empty chair, and laid on the couch, her arm over her eyes and her lips pursed in pain.

"I feel like shit," she mumbled.

"I'm gonna check the house," Alex said. "Do you want me to bring you water?"

"Yes, please," she whispered. "There's a bottle of pain relievers on the kitchen table. Could you bring me a couple of those too?"

"Will do."

He spent the next few minutes checking the house and locking the doors and windows, then stopped in the security office and looked at the newly installed cameras, making sure they were working properly. After he talked to Tiny, who was doing a perimeter check, Alex finished in the kitchen, filling a glass of water from the cooler in the corner. He snatched the bottle of pills from the table and dumped two into his hand. When he set it back down, he noticed a folded piece of paper with Miranda's name on it written in large, childlike handwriting.

Alex didn't like the feeling in his gut—the same one he had right before everything went to shit with

Melissa. Sick to his stomach, he picked up the paper and opened it.

You're not safe anywhere.

Chapter Nine

ALEX

"They're escalating, David," Alex said. "The note on the table was less than twenty-four hours after the text."

"Did the cameras pick up anything?" David asked. "Anyone unusual?"

"No one who wasn't supposed to be here. Miranda's manager, her assistant, her brother, the housekeeper, and two people working the grounds. Those two never came inside. Of course, it could have happened before the cameras were activated. I don't fucking know." He resisted the urge to chuck the nearest lamp across the room.

"Has there been any word on who sent the text?"

"Looks like it's a burner phone," Alex said and sighed, pushing a hand through his hair. "I've got Stan trying to run down where it was bought, but I'm not expecting much."

"How's Ms. Putnam?"

"Not good. No surprise. The one place she felt safe was her home. Now that's gone too. I'm, uh…I'm gonna stay with her. She doesn't want me to leave."

"That's a big switch from no bodyguard ever to keeping you overnight," David mused.

"She's scared, David. She said she feels safe when I'm here."

"Tell her you'll bring in more security."

"I tried," Alex said. "She agreed to it, but only if I stay. I don't want to say no."

Alex glanced across the foyer to the large living room. Miranda sat upright on the couch, stiff as a board, her eyes darting around the room every few seconds. Once he told her what he'd found, she'd foregone the water he'd grabbed and starting drinking glass after glass of scotch. He'd offered to walk her upstairs and wait while she got settled before he left, but she refused, shaking her head so hard her hair flew around her face.

"I don't want to be alone. I don't want to wonder who is outside, if the stranger I see is someone you sent or the crazy asshole out to get me. Can you stay? Please?"

Alex agreed. The fear on her face tore him to shreds. He wanted—no, needed—to keep her safe. He would do whatever he must to accomplish that.

"I'll send one of the boys to your place to get your clothes and stuff," David offered, pulling Alex's attention back to their conversation.

"There's a go bag in my office," he said. "Have somebody bring it over. They can call me when they get to the gate."

"No problem. It shouldn't be more than an hour. What about the press conference tomorrow?"

"They won't cancel," Alex grumbled. "Miranda called her manager, but Angela said the studio wouldn't budge. I want to bring in extra security. Can you set it up?"

"So since Ms. Putnam agreed to the additional security, you're going to run with it? You don't think she'll change her mind once it's daylight? You know they usually do."

"I don't think she will, not after tonight. Send the team list with my bag. I'll go over it, see how it looks, and break it to Miranda. She'll listen to me." Out of the corner of his eye, he saw Miranda get up and start pacing, glancing at him every few seconds. She was antsy. "I better go. I'll call you tomorrow."

Alex disconnected the call and shoved his phone in his pocket before crossing the foyer. Miranda had moved to the window, staring outside, gripping the scotch in her hand so tight her knuckles were white and the cubes rattled in the glass. He cleared his throat to get her attention.

She jumped, and the glass fell from her hand, bouncing across the carpet. She bent to grab it, but he reached it first, scooping it off the floor and setting it on the low coffee table. Fortunately, it only had the ice cubes in it.

The tight smile on her face didn't reach her eyes. After finding the note, he'd forgotten about her headache. The pain was clear in every line of her body. He didn't know how she stayed upright.

Alex reached for her, his every instinct screaming to comfort her. He hesitated, but she didn't, falling into his arms and burying her face against his chest. She sighed and wrapped her hands around the lapels of his jacket.

"You should get some sleep," he said, hugging her and gently patting her back. He closed his eyes. *Christ, what am I doing?*

"Are you staying?" she asked, her voice muffled against his chest.

He nodded. "I'll crash on the couch. One of the guys is bringing me a bag."

Miranda shook her head before he'd even finished speaking. She took a step back and looked at him, still gripping his jacket. "You can stay in the room across the hall from mine. It's a guest room with an attached bathroom."

"It's okay. I'll be fine down here." Staying across the hall from her, being that close to her, was not a good idea. Not when she was so vulnerable. He was already having trouble concentrating on his job as it was. "I'll be right here if you need me. I'll give you my number, so you can call or text me. It'll be okay."

Her hands fell away, her shoulders slumped, and the dejected look on her face tore his heart to shreds.

"Please, Alex? I...I won't feel safe if you're so far away. What if the person who left the note is still in the house?"

"We searched everywhere," he said. "No one is here. I promise."

She twisted her hands in front of her and stared at the floor. "Please? I won't bug you, I promise. I'll sleep better if you're across the hall."

He couldn't tell her no; he just couldn't.

"Okay."

Chapter Ten

MIRANDA

Every sound made Miranda jump, and every shadow held an unseen threat. When Cooper knocked on her door a few minutes after midnight, she screamed, bringing Alex into the hall and Tiny charging up the stairs.

"Sorry, sorry," she apologized and stepped around Cooper into the hallway, her hands up to calm her protective bodyguards. "I wasn't expecting my brother to knock. I'm okay."

Alex relaxed and nodded at Tiny before going back into his bedroom without a word. Miranda scowled, spun on her heel, and returned to her room.

Cooper followed her, confused. "What the hell is going on? There's like five people outside. I got stopped three times before I got in the house. What happened?"

She explained the threatening note Alex found in the kitchen and the subsequent addition of security staff. Cooper crossed his arms and glared at her.

"Now will you take it seriously?" he demanded. "Someone was in the house, Mermaid. They could have killed you."

"They didn't, though." She sighed. "And before you say anything else or yell at me again, I am taking it seriously. I agreed to more security. Alex is staying across the hall, and I'm going to do whatever my bodyguard and the security company says, no questions asked."

"It's about time. Now I won't worry while I'm in San Diego."

"San Diego? What for?"

"The Scorchers want me to try out. I got a call a couple of hours ago."

Miranda hugged her brother. The Scorchers were the hottest soccer team in the United States, and they wanted her little brother. Proud didn't accurately describe how she felt. She swiped away a tear before stepping back and smiling at him.

"Coop, that's great," she gushed. "It's your dream come true."

"It will be if I make the team." He kissed his sister on the cheek and headed for the door. "I gotta get to bed; my plane leaves early in the morning." Cooper stopped, his hand on the doorknob. "You need to sleep too. Promise me you'll try."

She nodded. "I promise."

Miranda didn't sleep, though. After Cooper left, she paced circles around the room for an hour. Her hair stood on end from running her fingers through it, her makeup was smudged, and her head throbbed like it was in a vise. Sleep was elusive. She wasn't sure she'd ever sleep again.

She'd been able to brush away the death threats, play them off as nothing when it had been a note, an email, or a phone call. But in the last two days, someone had shot at her and invaded her home. She was terrified. Terrified for herself, her brother, and her friends. Anyone around her could get hurt.

Even with Alex in the room across the hall, she was a bundle of nerves. If he was here, next to her, his intimidating presence holding the demons at bay, maybe she could relax and sleep.

Miranda threw herself on the bed, pulled the blanket around her shoulders, and hugged her pillow to her chest. She closed her eyes, her mind drifting to the hug from Alex. Thinking about it helped her relax; her eyes drifted closed and the muscles in her neck loosened, the tension easing a little. She hated how this madness in her life made her weak and out of control. She didn't want to be the damsel in distress while Alex played the knight in a tight, blue suit.

The window rattled, startling her. She jumped out of bed, tripped over the edge of the blanket, and stumbled across the room to the door. Before she knew what was happening, she found herself in front of the guest room door, knocking on the thick oak door with a trembling hand. Too late to take it back.

The door flew open as if Alex had been standing there waiting for her.

"Miranda? Everything okay?"

"Can I come in?" she whispered.

He nodded, stepping back and opening the door wider. He was more relaxed than she'd ever seen him. His jacket and bowtie were off, along with his shoes. The sleeves of his white shirt were rolled up, his tattooed forearms on full display. They wrapped around his wrists and onto the back of his hands. Miranda suspected it would take hours to discover all of them and couldn't help but wonder where else he might have tattoos.

Alex set his glass of amber liquid onto the table beside the bed and gestured for her to sit down. She perched on the side of the bed, staring at her feet, the heavy, oppressive silence suffocating her.

"Miranda?" he prodded.

The tears threatened to spill down her cheeks, and it made her want to scream. Sitting here made her vulnerable. She didn't want Alex to feel sorry for her. She closed her eyes and took a deep breath.

"Can I stay here for a while? I don't want to be alone."

Alex shrugged one shoulder and stared at a spot over her right shoulder. "If you want to stay, I won't say no. It *is* your house." He sat across from her on the edge of the chair, his elbows on his knees, hands folded in front of him.

"I bet you get this a lot, huh?"

Alex shot her a look, his sky blue eyes confused.

"I mean, in your line of work," she clarified. "Damsels in distress whining in your room."

"Can't say this has ever happened before." He chuckled, shaking his head. He exhaled like he'd been holding his breath. "You *are* allowed to whine, you know that, right? Life handed you a steaming pile of shit, Miranda. I certainly wouldn't expect you to be laughing and smiling. You're entitled to your feelings, every one of them. You can be afraid, whine, cry, scream, bitch, or even drink until you're falling-down drunk. If you wanted to, you could hide in the house for the next six months, ignoring everyone and everything in your life until the pain eats you alive, until you suffocate under the strain of it and the only choices you have left are to call it quits and let the pain win or shove it down deep, wrestle it into its cage, and go back to your life, faking it until you make it, or until a bullet misses its mark and takes you out."

"Alex?"

"What?" he snapped, as if he'd forgotten she was there.

"What happened to you?"

"Nothing," he grumbled, crossing his arms over his substantial chest, glowering at a spot on the wall more interesting than her.

"Is that what you're doing? Are you waiting to take a bullet and die?"

Alex shook his head and sighed. He pursed his lips and mumbled something incoherent under his breath. He scrubbed a hand over his face and looked her in the eye for the first time since she'd entered his room.

"You can stay as long as you want." He sat back, propped his feet on the edge of the bed, and closed his eyes.

Miranda stared at him, this huge beast of a man who seemed so perfect, so invincible, so put-together, but exuded a vulnerability she couldn't quite figure out. What was going on in his head? What happened to him to make him chase death? She lay down facing him and adjusted the blanket until she was comfortable. She kept her eyes on Alex until she drifted off to sleep.

Chapter Eleven

ALEX

He couldn't stop the bleeding. The blood poured out of her, staining her sensible white top. It dripped onto the ugly carpet beneath her and blended in with the red swirl pattern.

"Dammit, Melissa, don't do this. Do not do this."

Hands closed around his upper arm and tried to pull him away—tried to stop him from saving her.

"Melissa. Melissa!"

She didn't answer him. He closed his eyes and prayed for the last time in his life.

"Melissa!"

"Alex! Alex, wake up!"

He shot upright in his chair, his feet hitting the ground, his dead wife's name on his lips. Miranda kneeled beside him, gently shaking him.

"I'm sorry," she said, "but you were yelling and thrashing around."

"Um, no…no, it's okay. It was a nightmare—an old one I haven't had in a while." He ran a hand over his face, trying to wipe away the lingering pain and fear.

Miranda rose to her feet, keeping her blanket pulled tight around her shoulders. "Who's Melissa?"

Alex shook his head. "Miranda—"

"You don't have to talk about it if you don't want to," she said, sitting on the edge of the bed. "But I thought, you know, I'm here, you're here, and I make a good sounding board. You've mentioned Melissa's name a few times. I assume she's important to you."

Alex grabbed his empty scotch glass from the table, refilled it, and downed it in two swallows, relishing the burn as it traveled down his throat. He scrubbed the back of his hand over his lips and exhaled, his eyes pricking with tears. He hadn't talked about Melissa in two years, not since her death. Not with his brothers or his parents, not with the crisis counselor at work, nor the therapist David made him see. He wouldn't talk about her, no matter how much they pressured him.

"Melissa's my wife."

"You're married." It wasn't a question.

He swallowed past the lump in his throat. "I'm sorry. Melissa *was* my wife," he clarified. "She passed away a couple years ago."

"Oh." Miranda picked at the edge of the blanket. "I'm so sorry. Was she who you were dreaming about?"

He opened his mouth to tell her it was none of her business and to go back to sleep because he didn't want to talk about it. Not now, not ever. But something else came out.

"Every night I wake up with the image of Melissa covered in blood burned into the back of my eyelids. I hear her struggling to breathe and feel her fingers digging into my arms as she tries to hold on. I see the light fade from her eyes." He pinched the bridge of his nose, angry with himself, angry that the wall he'd carefully built over the years had come crumbling down so easily, knocked over by a woman he'd known for less than three days.

"What happened to her?"

"They shot her," Alex said.

"Oh my god, I'm so sorry. Who? How?"

"I…I don't like to talk about this." He sighed. "I never talk about it. With anyone."

"I'm a good listener, Alex. I promise I'll just listen. I won't say anything. Not one word." She pretended to zip her lips and pointed at the chair he'd vacated.

He shook his head; he didn't want to sit. He poured another glass of scotch, gripping it tightly in his left hand. He couldn't explain why, but he wanted to tell Miranda what happened. Maybe it would help her understand why he acted the way he did.

"We were on a job, me and Melissa. We'd been partners for a couple of years before we fell in love and got married." Miranda gave him a funny look. He knew what she was thinking. "Not exactly protocol, putting a husband and wife together on a job, but we made a great team. We were so in sync it was scary. After we got married, David kept us together.

We were in the field, on our last assignment together. David had promoted Melissa. She was my boss. We were going to start a family once she got the hang of her new job. Primetime assigned us to guard an actress who was receiving death threats from an old high school classmate. She was stubborn, didn't want a bodyguard. Kind of like you."

Miranda opened her mouth but snapped it closed and shrugged, a funny smile on her face. She mouthed "sorry" and gestured for him to continue.

"Anyway, we'd been working as her bodyguards for two months and nothing had happened. Courtney, the actress, was getting more difficult to deal with, especially since nothing had happened. One night, she ditched us, and it took hours to find her. Melissa found out she was at a party and went after her. I stayed in the car. Courtney hated me, and Melissa figured she'd be difficult if I was there. Melissa was escorting her out of the building, cutting through one of the banquet rooms, when gunfire and screams erupted." He stopped to take a breath, the lump in his throat making it hard to talk.

"By the time I got inside, it was too late. Courtney was hiding behind an overturned table, and Melissa was on the ground. Courtney said Melissa pushed her out of the way and took the bullets for her. They hit her three times—two in the chest, one in the abdomen. She bled out before help arrived. They never found the shooter."

"It wasn't the guy stalking Courtney?" Miranda asked.

Alex shook his head. "No, he alibied out." He couldn't stand up anymore, couldn't hold up his own weight. He dropped to the end of the bed, his head in his hands and tears sliding down his face as his shoulders shook. "She died because I failed. It's my fault." He dragged in a stuttering breath. "I never should have let her go in alone. It should have been me."

Miranda grabbed his hand and dragged it off his face, forcing him to look at her. She rested her head on his shoulder. "Alex, you didn't kill her," she whispered.

"People have been telling me that for two years. Trying to convince me to stop punishing myself, telling me there was nothing I could have done differently. But they're wrong. I should have taken the bullets, not Melissa. She'd be alive right now if I had done my job. And I wouldn't be spending every day of my life wishing it had been me instead of her."

"Don't say that—"

Alex cut her off. "It's true. I failed the one person I never should have failed. If I had done what I was supposed to and taken the lead, my wife would be alive."

"What do you think you should have done?" Miranda asked. "You didn't know what was going to happen. You *couldn't* have. You did your job. And if you weren't here, who would protect me?"

"I'm not sure I should protect you," Alex said. "I can do the undemanding jobs where someone's life isn't in danger, but this job? I'm terrified I'm going to fuck it up and get you killed. I'm not sure I can keep you safe."

Miranda leaped off the bed, stood in front of him, and jabbed her finger into his chest. "God damn it, Alex, you are the only reason I feel safe right now and am not out of my mind with fear because I know you *will* keep me safe. I trust you to keep me safe."

He looked up at her, his mouth open to protest and argue with her, but he found his hands on her waist, pulling her body flush against his as his lips crashed into hers. He needed to feel alive again, to find something good in his life, something good inside of him.

Miranda is good.

Alex pulled her onto the bed, falling back onto the stack of pillows and jumbled blankets. He cupped her face in his hands, nibbled on her lower lip, and groaned when she opened her mouth to let him in. Her tongue danced with his, her arms sliding around his neck, her knees on either side of his hips. She tasted like raspberries and a hint of scotch, her lips soft and supple as they moved with his. She was a perfect fit, as if she was meant to be in his arms.

He lost himself in her—the taste of her on his lips and her body moving with his. The dark surrounded them, cutting them off from everything and letting them forget the shit happening in the world around them. The only things were the two of them. He ran his hands over her body, exploring her, memorizing every curve and inch. He caressed her, kissed her, held her, and let her into the part in his heart he'd closed off after Melissa's death.

Alex didn't know how long he held her, his body thrumming with need for her, wanting and not wanting her, his head and his heart battling for control of his feelings.

Miranda pushed herself to her knees, sitting back on his thighs, her hands gripping the hem of her shirt. He put his hands on hers, stopping her.

"Wait, Miranda. Not…not now, not like this. Let's take things slow, okay?"

She let go of her shirt, leaned over him, and rested her hands on the pillow on either side of his head, her lips on his. She rolled to her side, pulling him with her, and continued to kiss him. They lay tangled together, kissing, until they both fell asleep.

Chapter Twelve

MIRANDA

Miranda woke to the sound of distant, insistent pounding. She untangled herself from Alex's arms, slipped out of the bed, and eased out the door. Tara stood in front of her bedroom door, knocking.

"Tara."

Her friend swung around with a loud squeak. "What the hell?" she whisper-shouted, her eyes darting between Miranda's door and the door she'd come out of. "Why aren't you…what are you doing?"

"I was…I'm…uh…" She yanked the door closed behind herself. "Why are you pounding on my door?"

"You have to leave in an hour. The press conference, remember?"

"Shit, I forgot." Miranda pushed a hand through her hair. "Is there any way we can cancel?"

Tara shook her head. "You're the female lead, girl-friend. The studio executives will be furious if you back out of a press conference a week before the world premiere. Then the rumor train will start again, and they'll slap the 'difficult' label back on you. You are finally getting passed it too. I think canceling is a horrible idea."

Miranda moaned. "Damn it. Alright, give me, I don't know, forty-five minutes or an hour, and I'll be downstairs."

"Fine, but make it fast," Tara muttered. "Here." She shoved an enormous cup of coffee into Miranda's hands then hurried down the hall.

She waited until Tara was out of sight before she stepped back into Alex's bedroom. Alex sat on the edge of the bed, waiting. He rose to his feet when she came through the door and crossed his arms, staring at her. Huge, intimidating.

"We should talk about last night," he said.

Dammit, I won't let him scare me away.

"I guess we should, huh?" she agreed. She shifted from foot to foot and stared up at the giant of a man in front of her. "Are you sorry?"

Alex was quiet long enough for her to realize he *was* sorry about what happened between them. He opened his mouth then closed it again. He shook his head and sank to the bed.

"I don't want to be. I just…there's this chatter in my head, telling me things I don't want to hear," he admitted, his voice gruff and downright sexy. "There are things I need to figure out."

Miranda crossed the room, stepped between his legs, and kissed the corner of his mouth. "It's okay," she whispered, running her fingers through the hair on the top of his head. "I understand." Which she *did*; she hated it, but she understood. And if she had to, she would wait. She wasn't looking for anything serious with her bodyguard, anyway; he simply made for a pleasant distraction.

Maybe if I keep telling myself that, I'll eventually believe it.

Alex squeezed her waist. He stared down at her, and for a split second, Miranda thought he might change his mind. Instead, he looked at his watch. "You should get ready. You've got the press conference in an hour."

Miranda nodded, twisted away from him, grabbed her coffee, and stepped out the door. "Right. Press conference. What would I do without you and Tara keeping me on my toes? I'll see you downstairs."

Two seconds later, she was leaning against her closed bedroom door.

"Fuck," she muttered, banging her head on the door behind her.

What the hell am I doing? Am I falling for my bodyguard?

Whenever Alex was around, there was an anxious flutter deep in the pit of her stomach. It wasn't a crush, a passing fancy as her grandmother used to say, or even her lusting after Alex because he was so damn attractive. It felt right when she was with him like it was meant to be.

Three days. I've known the man for three days.

She closed her eyes and inhaled. His scent was all over her, bringing back memories of last night. God, being with Alex was so good. Thinking about the kisses they'd shared, the comforting weight of his body on hers, and the way he touched her body made her tingle with intense desire.

Miranda resisted the urge to throw open the door, go back to Alex's room, and show him exactly why he shouldn't regret being with her. Instead, she peeled off her shirt and shorts, dropped them on the end of the bed, and made her way to the en-suite bathroom. She turned on the shower and checked her head wound in the mirror while she waited for the water to heat. The bruise had turned an ugly yellow color. It would take a shit-ton of makeup to cover.

The makeup wouldn't stop the questions, though. Today's press conference was going to be about the death threats she'd been receiving rather than her upcoming movie.

I can't wait.

Chapter Thirteen

ALEX

Alex closed the door behind Miranda and leaned against it, his palms flat on the hard oak, head hanging.

What the fuck am I doing? Getting close to a client, getting intimate with a client, letting her under my skin?

Once upon a time, he'd been the consummate professional until he threw those values away for a pain-in-the-ass, strikingly gorgeous actress who looked like his dead wife. He couldn't wrap his head around how he'd let it happen, how he'd fallen down this rabbit hole with a woman he'd known for three days. It didn't matter who she looked like. He never should have let it get this far.

He hadn't been lying when he told Miranda that chatter filled his head. He needed to work through his crazy, jumbled thoughts. He closed his eyes and took a deep breath. His head told him to stop, right now, before things went any further, regardless of the twisted, sick feeling in his gut screaming at him that it was a mistake to push her away. This woman could change his life for the better. He pushed those thoughts and feelings down deep, refusing to acknowledge them. He had a job to do—a job he planned to finish. Once it was over, he would decide what he wanted to do. Until then, it was business as usual.

Alex shoved away from the door and grabbed his go bag. He needed to clean up and change. He had a job to do.

Half an hour later, Alex was downstairs with Starbucks in his hand—courtesy of Tiny—checking the security monitors in the office. He heard Angela and Tara in the hall, joined a few seconds later by Miranda. They checked Miranda's agenda for the day before separating.

"Hey, what are you doing in here?" Miranda asked, sliding into the chair beside him. Her leg touched his, and her hand landed on his arm.

"I thought I'd go over the footage from yesterday again," Alex replied, rolling his chair away from her, putting a foot or so between them. He ignored the hurt look on her face and took a drink of his coffee, wincing when it burned his tongue.

"Did you find anything?" she asked.

"No. I don't think I'm going to, either." He checked his watch to avoid looking at Miranda. "We need to go, or you'll be late. I'll meet you out front." He shoved to his feet and hurried from the room, not bothering to wait for her answer or see if she followed him.

Alex yelled for Tiny, who came around the corner of the house and jogged to the driver's side of the car. Alex climbed in front and busied himself with his phone, ignoring Miranda when she came out the door. Tiny held the door open for her and her entourage, then climbed behind the wheel.

Thankfully, the car ride to the conference center was short. It didn't thrill Alex to have to endure Angela's constant chatter or the long, awkward side glances from Miranda.

He turned in his seat to steal a look at her, reminding himself again she was his client. He cleared his throat before he spoke.

"I want you to wait in the car with Tiny while I check things out. I have extra people from Primetime coming, and I want to brief them before we go in."

Angela scoffed. "We're late. We'll go in with you, and you can brief your team inside."

"No, Angie, I can wait in the car like Mr. Peters said," Miranda reassured Angela.

"But Mir—"

"Enough, Angie," Miranda interrupted. "I'll do what he said. What's the point of a bodyguard if I won't do what he asks? His job is to keep me safe. The least I can do is cooperate." She smiled at Alex. "Can Angie go in with you?"

"Sure," he said. No one was trying to kill her; his only concern was Miranda.

"Not so hard, right?" Miranda smiled at her friend. "Easier to ask to go with him than be difficult."

Angela rolled her eyes and snorted, clearly unhappy.

Alex turned around, chuckling under his breath. This was a first: a client who cooperated. This was one for the books.

As soon as the car stopped, he jumped out, yelling over his shoulder for Tiny to keep Miranda in the car as he sprinted up the stairs and through the double doors of the conference center. He might be struggling with his feelings for his client, but he knew how to do his job.

While the studio wouldn't agree to cancel the press conference, they did agree to tighten security and add metal detectors, bag searches, and extra security personnel at every door. It eased his worries a little. Alex only trusted his own people, which was why he had David send over additional staff.

The trio met him in the lobby while Angela stood off to one side, observing. David sent Stan, Primetime's resident tech genius and an MIT graduate; Donald, not exactly the bodyguard type—too gangly and awkward—but he was a good guy, loyal to a fault, and a hard worker trying to get field experience before David put him in a management position; and Jill, David's daughter and the muscle of the group. Alex dared anyone to fuck with Jill and come out of it alive. She hadn't earned the scar on her neck playing dolls. Someone had pulled a knife on her client and Jill charged after them. She dove between them, got the blade in her neck, and still took the guy down without flinching. David couldn't have sent a better group.

Stan distributed earpieces while Alex gave everyone a rundown of where he wanted them and what he wanted them doing. Angela leaned against the wall, checking her watch every few seconds and earning a dirty look from Jill.

"You got a problem?" she spat.

Angela shook her head, her brow furrowed and her lips set in a thin, tight line. "No. I'm good. I need you to guys to hurry things along, though. We're wasting time."

"I don't think keeping our client safe is a waste of time, do you?" Jill asked. She took a step toward Angela, her fists clenched and her back ramrod straight.

Angela had the common sense to back down. She ducked her head and mumbled, "No."

"That's what I thought," Jill snapped.

Alex put a hand on Jill's arm, trying to hold back the laughter as he told her to chill. She gave him one of her don't-fuck-with-me looks, turned on her heels, and made a beeline for her position by the door, not letting anyone or anything deter her. Stan followed her, muttering under his breath about scanning the auditorium.

"Come on, Donnie. You're with me," Alex said with a chuckle. "I want you to drive the SUV around the block a few times, then park in the lot a few blocks north. Tiny scouted the locale yesterday and determined it secure. I want Tiny with me when I take Ms. Putnam in the building."

Donald nodded. "Yes, sir."

"Are you bringing her in now?" Angela asked.

Alex nodded, which earned him a smile from Miranda's manager before she scurried off to God-knew-where. Probably off to inform the press. At least she'd be out of his hair for the next few minutes.

Donald trailed after him, looking like a lost puppy, though Alex knew if push came to shove, he'd do whatever needed to be done. They cut through the crowd out front to the SUV parked on the street. Alex opened the door, took Miranda's hand, and helped her out.

Miranda tucked her hand in the crook of his arm, and he led her inside, guiding her through the growing crowd. It seemed everyone had turned out for the press conference. They didn't wait to ask their questions, though; people shouted after her from every direction. He wanted to wrap his arm around her waist and hold her tight against his side—a completely unprofessional thought. His fingers itched with the need to touch her, to hold her hand, to pull her against his side. He had to remind himself again he was on the job.

I am seriously fucked.

Chapter Fourteen

MIRANDA

Miranda kept a tight hold on Alex's arm, her fingers digging into the powerful muscle. She was hyperaware of everything around her—every voice, every sound, *everything*. She concentrated on breathing, a ten count in and a ten count out. If it wasn't for Alex, she wasn't sure she would be able to do this.

Angela swooped in out of nowhere, her hands on her hips and an angry scowl on her face.

"The press knows."

"The press knows *what*?" Miranda inquired.

"They know someone broke into the house," Angela spat. "Someone talked." She glared at Alex.

An angry scowl appeared on Alex's face, far more attractive than Angela's. He grabbed Miranda's hand and squeezed; the gesture meant to comfort her.

"My people didn't talk," he snarled. "Dozens of people flit in and out of Ms. Putnam's house every day. It must have been one of them. Why don't you go find someone else to glare at and let me do my job?"

Alex wrapped an arm around Miranda's waist and guided her past Angela. He ignored her manager's irritated huff as he mounted the stairs and led Miranda to the back of the stage. Miranda glanced back over her shoulder, but to her surprise, Angie wasn't following them.

Miranda let Alex take the lead, following him as the stage manager pointed them to where he wanted them to stand. She hated these things, hated sitting and listening to people shout questions at her—most of them ridiculous, all of them repetitive. They never asked any new questions. It was the same ones a million times over, and they were never about the movie she was promoting. Her personal life was a favorite topic. The shooting and the rumors about her house being broken into would no doubt be the focus of the day. It wasn't going to be easy.

It didn't help she was a nervous wreck, thinking everyone was the person who wanted her dead. Every noise made her jump, and every flash from a camera startled her. She should have canceled. She wanted to go home.

The only reason she hadn't bolted was because Alex stood right behind her, so close she felt his breath on her neck and smelled the cologne he wore. Any minute they'd call her name, and she'd have to go out on the stage alone, without Alex.

I can't do it.

Miranda abruptly spun around and pushed Alex backward, her palms flat on his chest. She shoved him into a dark corner obscured by the stage curtain.

"I can't do this, Alex," she whispered. "I can't go out there and act normal, not when a crazy person is out to get me." Her heart pounded, and the blood raced through her veins. She was going to lose it. Her hands fisted in Alex's jacket as she tried to ground herself.

Alex grabbed her hands, held them at her side, and leaned over her, his insanely blue eyes boring into hers. "Look at me, Miranda. You can do this. I will be right here. I promise." He pointed to a spot near the curtain where she would be able to see him on stage. "I will stand right there, and I will not move. If you get nervous or need a second to collect your thoughts, look at me. And for God's sake, breathe. Okay?"

Miranda dragged in a deep breath and stared into his eyes, letting his proximity calm her. By the time they called her co-star's name, she thought she might be okay.

"You good?" Alex asked.

Miranda nodded. God, she wanted to wrap her arms around his neck and kiss him. But she respected his need to figure things out and didn't push him. Instead of kissing him, she gave him a tight smile.

"Thank you," she whispered, the words heavy with everything she wanted to say.

Her name echoed through the auditorium, her signal to join the other actors on stage. She plastered a smile on her face, turned, and jogged onstage.

Chapter Fifteen

ALEX

Alex couldn't take his eyes off Miranda. Despite what she said, she sat calmly on the stage, answering the press' ridiculous questions with grace and a smile. If it had been him, he would have lashed out.

It was the same feeling he had when the press tore Chris and Sofia apart. He wanted to destroy someone, rip them to shreds. His protective streak was why he made a damn good bodyguard. It had only failed him once.

He pushed the thought out of his head; thinking about his failures eroded his confidence and put Miranda in danger. He couldn't let that happen.

Forty-five minutes later, Miranda was off the stage and standing beside him, the two of them surrounded by his team, Angela, and Tara. He doled out another set of instructions and watched as the team scattered to do as they were told. Angela walked away, her phone pressed to her ear, while Tara went with Donnie and Tiny to get the car, leaving him and Miranda alone.

"I'm glad that's over," she breathed.

"You did great," he said. He stood a foot or so away from her, arms crossed over his chest, eyes on a movie poster over her shoulder. If he didn't look at her, maybe the urge to take her in his arms and kiss her senseless would go away.

"Are you okay?" Miranda whispered, easing closer to him. "Or did the chatter in your head finally get to you?"

Alex took a deep breath and shifted to his back foot in a poor attempt to put distance between them.

"Don't push me away, Alex," she begged, her blue eyes pleading with him. "Please, *please*, don't push me away."

He shrugged, unable to speak. It wasn't the answer she wanted, but he didn't know what to say. The thoughts in his head made no sense. How would he explain it to her?

"Please?" Miranda put her hand on the center of his chest and smiled up at him. "Talk to me. We can figure this out, but you have to talk to me."

Alex sighed and let his hand fall to her waist, squeezing gently. "I'm afraid anything I say will be the wrong thing. I am attracted to you, but I need to sort stuff out first, okay? It's complicated."

"My life is complicated." She sighed. "Too complicated. Why can't this be easy?"

"Unfortunately, this is far from easy. I can't explain right now, but I will, I promise."

How the hell do I tell her she looks like my dead wife?

Miranda nodded and kissed his cheek. "That's all I can ask. Thank you."

"Well, shit," someone bellowed from Alex's left. "I wish my clients were as thankful as you."

Alex released Miranda with a sigh and turned to see Brady Gaither a few feet away, a nasty, cat-that-swallowed-the-canary smile on his face.

"Son of a bitch," Alex muttered.

Miranda squeezed Alex's arm, her eyes half-closed as she watched Gaither approach. "Who is that?"

"A guy I used to work with."

"He gives me the creeps," she mumbled as Gaither came to a stop in front of them.

Alex turned around and stepped in front of Miranda, shielding her with his body. "Hey, Brady. You working this gig too?" he asked, reaching to shake Gaither's hand while doing his best to keep himself between Miranda and Gaither. Revulsion rolled off her in waves.

"Yeah," Gaither responded, waving at the crowd of celebrities on the other side of the stage without indicating which celebrity he meant. "Ms. Putnam, it's an honor to meet you. I'm a big fan of your work." He smiled his familiar, leering grin and held out his hand.

Miranda didn't say a word. She ignored his out-stretched hand, smiled, and nodded, her hand on Alex's arm tightening until her nails dug into the muscle. Disgust and irritation crossed Gaither's face at her obvious slight, and his lips pursed, one eyebrow raised. He turned to Alex as his eyes flashed with something odd.

"I guess I can see why you'd fuck her, Alex," Gaither said, his voice so low only he and Miranda could hear it. "Because you two are fucking, right?"

"Gaither—" The threat in Alex's voice was clear, and Gaither knew him well enough to recognize it. It didn't seem to matter because Gaither was determined to say his piece.

"Does David know you're fucking a client?" Gaither jeered. "He must not, or he'd fire your self-righteous, pompous ass like he fired me."

Alex clenched his fist but resisted the urge to use it on Gaither. He wouldn't make a scene where Miranda's colleagues might see or hear a confrontation. He was a professional.

"You're an ass, Gaither," Alex snarled. "Excuse us." He turned his back on Brady Gaither, took Miranda's arm, and led her out the back of the auditorium.

"What is that guy's problem?" Miranda hissed, looking over Alex's shoulder as he pushed her down the hallway.

"He hates me." Alex shrugged. "A lot." He hurried toward a door with an exit sign over it, Miranda's hand in his. He shoved open the door and looked both ways, trying to get his bearings through the bright sun burning his eyes.

He yanked his cell phone from his pocket, but before he could dial, it rang in his hand.

"Peters."

"Alex, where are you?" Tiny sounded pissed and out of breath.

"Behind the conference center. Bring the car around back; I don't want to take Ms. Putnam out front."

"Yeah, about the car…"

Alex closed his eyes. "What happened to the car?"

Tiny paced in front of the vandalized SUV, uttering curses under his breath. The large, black Escalade was a mess. It sat on four flat tires, "bitch" scrawled across the windshield in red paint, along with "stay home" and "I warned you" scratched into the hood. It had two broken windows, red paint and deep key scratches covering the doors and back.

As soon as Tiny told him what happened, Alex put Miranda and Tara in a car with Jill and Donnie. He gave them strict instructions to take the girls straight back to the mansion and stay with them until he got there.

Miranda tried to argue and demanded to see the car, but Alex cut her off with a stern look, escorted her to Jill's car, and sent them away without another word. She was pissed, but Alex didn't care. Especially since seeing the vehicle.

"How the fuck did this happen?" he demanded.

Tiny shook his head, an indistinguishable growl leaving him. Alex hadn't seen him this pissed in a long time. "I don't fucking know. Donnie parked exactly where we told him. No one knew where the damn car was except us. When I came out to get it, I found this."

Alex scrubbed a hand over his face. "Somebody is talking. Angela was right."

"It's not anybody from Primetime," Tiny said. "It can't be."

"It has to be," Alex snapped. "Find out who it is. And tighten security. Everything from here on out is kept between you and me. I'll loop people in when necessary."

"Understood. And don't worry, boss. I will find out who did this." Another stream of curses fell from Tiny's lips, and he kicked one of the flat tires.

"Hey, you remember Brady Gaither?" Alex asked.

Tiny nodded. "Yeah. Used to work for David."

"Right. Do me a favor and find out if he's on the job right now and, if so, who it's with. Find out if he's independent or working with a company. Then figure out how this happened to the car. It better not be anybody from Primetime, or I'll kill them. Call somebody to get this out of here and get us a replacement."

"On it, boss."

Alex dropped to the curb, his head in his hands. He was supposed to leave tomorrow for Chris and Sofia's wedding. Given everything Miranda had endured the last three days, telling her would not go over well. While he trusted his team with his life and Miranda's as well, she wasn't going to like the idea of him leaving for the weekend. He dreaded the thought of telling her.

When he agreed to take this job, taking the weekend off to go to Chris and Sofia's wedding hadn't been an issue. Now, he was emotionally invested in not only the job but his client as well. He wasn't sure he could leave her, even for only three days. It was a conversation he didn't want to have, but it needed to be done.

"Tiny!"

"Yeah, boss?"

"What's the ETA on the new car? I need to talk to our client."

Chapter Sixteen

MIRANDA

Alex dumped Miranda and Tara in a car with the skinny, nervous guy and the scary blonde with the scar on her neck and ordered them to take her home. He wouldn't answer any of her questions. She didn't like the look on his face as he stalked across the parking—anger, irritation, confusion. She watched him through the window until the car rounded the corner, and he was out of sight.

Back home, Jill escorted Miranda and Tara inside, refused Miranda's offer of a drink, and headed to the security office to join Donnie. Miranda followed, stopping in the doorway to stare at the monitors for a few seconds. They covered every inch of the house and grounds except bedrooms and bathrooms. She sighed and cleared her throat.

Donnie turned and smiled at her. "Can I help you, Ms. Putnam?"

"Do you know when Mr. Peters will be back?"

"I'm sorry, no. Jill?"

Jill looked up and shrugged. "Later, I guess."

"If you see him before I do, please tell him I need to speak with him," Miranda said.

"Sure, whatever." Jill turned back to the monitors, dismissing Miranda.

Miranda needed to talk to Alex. She would demand he tell her everything. It was her life, and she had a right to know what was going on. Hiding things from her wasn't an option. She wanted full disclosure from now on.

Miranda returned to the kitchen and Tara, who wanted to discuss the calendar for the upcoming weekend. Miranda wasn't in the mood, so she brushed her assistant off, grabbed a bottle of water, and headed for the enormous family room at the back of the house.

The family room was her favorite room in the house. It was the first she renovated when she bought the place. It overlooked the backyard with its Olympic-sized pool and gorgeous gardens. It was a formal dining room before she remodeled. She knew she wouldn't use it for its intended purpose, so she hired a decorator to turn it into a comfortable room for hanging out. She filled it with big, overstuffed chairs and couches, a big screen TV, and a mini fridge. When she wanted to forget the rest of the world existed, she hid in the family room.

Miranda sank onto the huge couch and pulled a blanket over her legs. Another headache pulsed behind her eyes. She held the cold water bottle against her head and closed her eyes.

She was desperate for a break from the insanity. If only she could sneak away for the weekend. Maybe she would have Tara cancel her weekend stuff and hide out in her bedroom until Monday.

"Ms. Putnam?"

The deep, sexy voice rocked her to her core and sent tingles racing up and down her spine.

"I think you can call me Miranda. Especially after last night," she mumbled.

Alex chuckled. "Okay, Miranda."

"Are you going to tell me what happened to the Escalade? Tara only got a glimpse, but she said it was bad."

"I guess." He unbuttoned his jacket and shoved his hands in his pocket. "Someone vandalized it. We suspect it was your stalker."

"Oh." Miranda swallowed and squeezed her eyes closed. She pulled her legs up and wrapped her arms around them. She rested her chin on her knees and stared at Alex. "So he's a stalker now, huh?"

"I think it's safe to assume so," he said. "I'm sorry."

She snorted. "What are you sorry for?"

"I'm sorry you're going through this. I'm sorry you're scared. And I'm sorry I can't do more to make you safe."

Her eyes filled with tears, and she bit her lip to keep from crying. "I'm only safe when I'm with you," she whispered.

"Well, shit. That doesn't make what I have to say any easier." He sat on the ottoman in front of her. "I have to talk to you."

Miranda nodded. "Okay."

"It's about this weekend." He leaned closer, his elbows on his knees and his hands folded in front of him.

Miranda stared at them—big, powerful hands with thick fingers, patient and gentle. She longed to have them touch her again, caress her skin, dig into her muscles, and hold her close. She swallowed back the moan of desire rising in her throat and forced a smile onto her face.

"First things first, how do you like Jill and Donnie?" he asked.

Miranda shrugged. "They're okay, I guess. Why?"

"They'll be here this weekend with Tiny. He's going to be running things Friday, Saturday, and Sunday. They'll be helping him, so I wanted to make sure you're comfortable with them. I'll be back Monday morning."

"Wait? What do you mean you'll be back on Monday? You won't be here? Where are you going?" She heard the panic in her voice and hated it, but she couldn't control it.

"I have to go out of town. It was in the paperwork the security firm sent you. This weekend, you'll have a different security team until I get back."

"No. You can't," she snapped. "You're working for me. Cancel it."

Alex pursed his lips and shook his head. He rubbed his temples with two fingers. "Miranda, please don't be difficult."

She sighed. "I'm sorry, Alex. I know I'm being a bitchy, snotty brat, but I...I don't want anyone else. I want *you*. You're the only reason I even feel safe. You can't leave me. Especially after the car, and the note, and the shooting." She dug her nails into her thighs and struggled to catch her breath. "Please?"

Alex shook his head. "This isn't up for discussion. One of my best friends is getting married. I can't miss it. Chris and his fiancée had a rough time, but they came through it, and I want to be there to help them celebrate. I'm sorry, Miranda, I am, but I will not let them down." He pushed himself to his feet, put his hand on her shoulder, and squeezed. "Tiny's a good man and a terrific bodyguard. You'll be fine."

Miranda stared after him, unable to speak. She didn't want him to go. She tried to tell herself it was because she was safe with him protecting her, but it was so much more. She wanted Alex with her all the time.

"What if I go with you?" she blurted.

He stopped in the doorway, one foot in the family room and one foot in the hallway. He froze for a split second before turning back to look at her.

"What did you say?"

Miranda jumped to her feet, grabbing the back of the couch when the blood rushed to her head and a wave of dizziness washed over her. "I could go with you. You said it's a wedding, right? Let me be your plus one. Your date."

Alex crossed his arms over his chest and scowled. "My date?" he grumbled in his deep, sexy voice.

She didn't like his scowl, but she'd gone this far, so she might as well go all the way. "I mean…I wouldn't *really* be your date. We'd know it was strictly business."

"You've got a photo shoot on Saturday, the brunch thing on Sunday—"

"I'll move them," she interrupted. "Please, Alex, at least think about it. I'm terrified to leave the house without you. I'm terrified to go outside. If you're not here, I'm not sure I'll be able to go to the photo shoot or the brunch anyway."

"Then cancel and hunker down here until I get back," he said. "God knows it would make security's job easier."

"Please, Alex, say yes. When I'm with you, I *know* I'm safe."

Alex sighed and stepped back into the room. "I guess we can discuss it."

"I think we just did. Please say yes. I promise to be on my best behavior. I'll leave my snotty actress persona at home." She gave him a weak smile.

Alex snorted and laughed. "You can bring it. It'll go well with my brother and Chris's holier-than-thou attitudes."

"Does that mean yes?" Miranda asked.

He pushed a hand through his hair, making it both messy and sexy. She longed to run her fingers through it.

"Alex?"

He nodded. "Okay. Clear your schedule for the weekend." He turned to go but stopped at the door. "By the way, you can't tell anyone where you're going. It's a private ceremony."

"I promise. I won't say a word to anyone, and I'll be on my best behavior." She pretended to lock her lips and threw away the imaginary key.

Alex laughed and shook his head. "I can't wait to see that."

Chapter Seventeen

ALEX

W *hat the hell was I thinking?*
The problem was he wasn't. He'd agreed to take his client away for the weekend. David would kill him.

"I think it's a great idea," David said when Alex called to tell him. "Especially after everything that's happened. I'll feel better if she's with you for the weekend."

"Okay..." He hadn't expected David to agree with his plan.

"Let's keep it under wraps, though. Strictly need to know. We'll say she's staying in for the weekend, taking a break because of the recent threats to her life. We'll keep the team in place, pretend she's home." David was on a roll. "Maybe we can draw the asshole out. If he thinks she's home, maybe he'll try to break in, and we can catch him."

"Whatever you say, boss." As long as Miranda wasn't in danger, Alex didn't care what they did.

Thank God he's not angry.

David prattled on about brilliant ideas and Alex being indispensable, blah, blah, blah. He cleared his throat, cutting David off mid-sentence.

Definitely not angry.

"So, we're good?" Alex asked.

"Damn right we are," David replied. "Tell Chris and Caleb I said hi."

The line disconnected, leaving Alex wondering what the hell he had done to deserve David as a boss. Anyone else would have lost their shit and most likely accused him of sleeping with Miranda. It was a logical assumption, especially since he was taking her out of town, alone.

His next call was to Tiny, the only other person he planned to tell. To his surprise, Tiny took it in stride.

"No problem, boss. I'll clear out the house and keep the team in place, but outside. I'll tell them Ms. Putnam is desperate for privacy, and we are to stay out of the house for the weekend. If we're not inside, it will make it easy to keep everyone else out. Don't worry. I'll take care of everything. You go have fun with your friends. Hopefully, the spitfire behaves herself."

Alex chuckled. Spitfire was an accurate description of Miranda. "Thanks, Tiny. You're a good guy."

"Yeah, well, I'm glad you think so. Tell David, okay? I could use a raise."

They said their goodbyes, and Tiny assured him he'd take care of everything. Alex planned to follow through with a good evaluation. A superb one. Tiny deserved it.

He tossed his phone aside, zipped up his duffel bag, and stretched out on the bed. He wanted to push the doubts regarding Miranda out of his head, cross the hall, and try to make things work with her.

But doubt glued him in place. He still wasn't sure his feelings for Miranda were genuine or because of her resemblance to Melissa. Until he figured it out, he needed to keep himself in check.

So why did he agree to let her tag along to the wedding?

Because I enjoy torturing myself.

Alex put an arm over his eyes and tried not to dwell on the upcoming weekend.

———————————————

Miranda peered out the Tahoe's window. "This is gorgeous."

"It is, isn't it? Chris bought it six, seven months ago. He wanted to get out of the city." He drove around the side of the house and parked. He cut the engine and turned to Miranda. "Look, I have to tell you something."

She scrunched up her nose, which he found adorable. He did his best to ignore it; he didn't want to get distracted. It happened far too easily when he was alone with Miranda. The three-hour drive from the city had taken a Herculean effort on his part to stay focused.

"Okay." She drew the word out.

"I probably should have told you this sooner, but my friend is Chris Chandler."

Miranda's eyes widened, and she sat up straight in her seat. "Chris Chandler? The same Chris Chandler who was all over Gossip Monger a few months ago because he dated a hooker?"

Alex rolled his eyes and tried to keep his irritation in check. "Sofia was *not* a hooker. She was a professional escort, a companion. You obviously haven't heard the whole story. She is an amazing woman who Chris loves very much. Whatever you do, do not utter the word 'hooker' anywhere near Chris. Please try to remember these people are my friends, and they mean a lot to me." His tone was harsh, but he wouldn't allow anyone to hurt Chris and Sofia. They'd been through enough.

"I'm sorry," Miranda said, eyes downcast. "I should know better. I'm the last person who should judge anybody based on a gossip rag's website."

"They've been through hell, and they didn't deserve it. It's still difficult for them. Every time they go anywhere or do anything, the inevitable question about Sofia's former profession as an escort comes up. I don't want it invading their wedding. Mum's the word. Okay?"

"I won't say a word, I swear. This weekend is important to you, huh?"

"Yes, it is." He sighed. "We're close. I've been Chris's bodyguard for almost two years. I went to work for him shortly after Melissa's death. He's always been good to me. This weekend is important them, and I want it to be perfect."

Miranda raised her right hand and smiled at him, her turquoise eyes filled with mischief. "I will be on my best behavior. I told you—I'll check my diva attitude at the door."

Alex laughed. "Thank God. I'm not sure I can handle three crazy actors this weekend."

"Three?"

"Oh, yeah, um, my brother is here too. He and Chris are friends. He's the reason I work for Chris. His manager, Paul, is Chris's manager. Paul met me when I worked for my brother and when Chris needed a bodyguard, he came to me for help."

Miranda's nose scrunched up again. If she didn't stop, he was going to kiss her.

"Who's your brother?"

"Caleb Peters."

Miranda pushed a hand through her hair, giving it a messy bedhead look. It reminded him of how she looked after they'd spent the night together. He took a deep breath. He needed to focus.

"How the hell did I not know? Is that what you meant when you said they have attitudes? They're actors? Wow, you're full of secrets, aren't you? I worked with Caleb a few years ago."

Alex nodded. "He mentioned it when I told him you were coming."

"Do they know I'm your client?"

"Yes. Well, Chris and Caleb do. To everyone else, you're the pretty actress who agreed to be my date."

"I guess I have to pretend I like you." Miranda winked and giggled. "Thank God I'm an actress."

"You're a riot," he said with a smirk. "But, yes, you do need to pretend to like me. Remember, this is a party. Try to enjoy yourself."

"I'm looking forward to this. No one knows where I am. No one knows what I'm doing. It's kind of nice."

"You didn't tell anybody where we were going? Not even Angela or Tara?"

"You told me not to," she reminded him. "I didn't even tell Cooper. Fortunately, he's in San Diego at a tryout for the Scorchers, so no third degree from my brother. He won't be back until Tuesday. No one knows where I am."

Alex tried not to look surprised, but he must have failed miserably because Miranda smacked him on the arm and gave him a dirty look.

"Stop it. I can behave when I have to. I promised I wouldn't tell, and I didn't."

"I'm impressed. Thank you." Alex pushed open his car door. "Come on. Let's go meet everyone."

Miranda met him at the back of the Escalade, took his hand, and let him lead her onto the porch. He tapped twice on the door before pushing it open.

"Hello?" he called. "It's Alex!"

"We're back here!"

Oliver, Chris' black and white Border Collie, flew around the corner, slid to a stop in front of Alex, and stared up at him, his tale thumping against the floor.

"Hey, Ollie." Alex dropped Miranda's hand and crouched in front of the dog. "How you been? You been a good boy?"

Oliver stared at Alex with his big brown eyes, a doggie grin on his face. Miranda kneeled beside Alex and held her hand out to the dog, palm down.

"Who is this cutie?" she asked.

"This is Oliver, Chris's dog. He's a sweetheart. And the ring bearer."

Miranda burst out laughing, and Alex's heart swelled. God, it was good to hear her laugh.

"Seriously? The ring bearer?" She giggled.

"Yep," Alex said, rising to his feet. "He'll do a great job too."

They went looking for Chris, Sofia, and Alex's brother, Caleb. They found them with Chris's best friend, Seth, and Chris's parents on the back patio that ran the length of the house. As soon as Alex and Miranda stepped through the door, Oliver at their side, Sofia bounded to her feet and threw her arms around him, hugging him tight.

"Alex!" she squealed. "I'm so glad to see you!"

Alex kissed Sofia's cheek and hugged her back. She was a bright ray of sunshine in the world and the perfect woman for Chris. It thrilled him his friend had found an amazing woman to love. He and Sofia had become good friends over the last few months.

Within seconds, his friends, people he had come to think of as family, surrounded him. His brother was right there in the mix, slapping him on the back, and teasing him for taking so long to drive up.

He was so consumed with greeting his loved ones that he almost forgot Miranda was there until Sofia called his name again.

"Oh my god, Alex! You neglected to tell me you were bringing *Miranda Putnam* to my wedding."

Sofia stood beside Miranda, clasping her hand, a huge grin on her face. Miranda shrugged one shoulder and smiled at him.

"I take it you know my date, then?" he asked.

"Uh, yeah." Sofia laughed. "I'm sorry, Ms. Putnam. I'm a huge fan. I love your movies."

"Please, call me Miranda."

Chris swooped in and pulled Sofia into his arms. "Sof, you act like you've never been around a celebrity before." He chuckled.

"Oh god, I'm being an idiot," Sofia said. "Sorry. Thank you so much for coming."

"Thank you for having me." Miranda smiled and took Alex's hand. She turned to Chris. "It's nice to meet you, Chris. I've heard a lot about you."

"I'm sure you have." Chris rolled his eyes. "Don't believe everything you read."

"Ditto," Miranda said. "I'd appreciate it you afforded me the same courtesy." She peered around the broad-shouldered actor. "Caleb, it's good to see you too."

Caleb waved at Miranda before he shot a questioning look at his brother and Miranda's clasped hands. Alex mouthed, *Not now.*

Alex finished the introductions, grabbed a couple of beers, and sat on one of the patio chairs. Miranda perched beside him, spinning her beer bottle in her hand and picking at the label.

"You okay?" he asked.

"Mm-hm," she hummed. "I'm a little out of my element. It's nerve-wracking being around people you don't know well. And the pressure of being at a wedding for someone you've never met—"

Alex squeezed her hand. "You'll be fine. You're resilient; you can handle it." He looked around. "Would you like to go for a walk? The view of the lake is gorgeous."

She nodded. "Yes, please."

Alex held her hand as they walked past everyone and down the stairs. He stopped long enough to tell Caleb they were going for a walk before guiding Miranda to the well-worn path leading to the lake.

They passed a large houseboat tied to a dock and followed the path along the lake. There was a large rock outcropping a few hundred yards along the path. It afforded a gorgeous view of the lake. Alex had discovered it a month earlier when he visited Chris and Sofia, and he wanted to show it to Miranda.

"If we climb up there, we'll get a superb view of the lake," he said, pointing to the outcropping.

Miranda wiped her hands on her jeans. "Alright, let's go." She pulled her hand from Alex's, and before he could stop her, she started climbing the rock outcropping.

Alex tried to grab her arm, but she was too fast. "Hold up. We'll walk around and take the path on the other side."

"C'mon, slowpoke," she called over her shoulder. "This is easy. I could do it in my sleep."

The words were barely out of her mouth before she let out a startled squeal. Alex watched in horror as she slid off the rocks, scrambling for something to grab.

"Shit!" Alex instinctively stepped closer and held out his arms. It might not do any good, but it didn't matter because he had to try something.

Miranda landed on him, and they fell to the ground with a grunt, Alex's head bouncing off the ground and knocking into hers.

"Ow," she moaned, rolling off him and onto her back, her hand pressed to her forehead.

Alex hovered over her, eyes roving over her, checking for injuries.

"Are you okay?"

"My head hurts," she complained. "My hands hurt." She squinted at him. "You're truly my hero, Alex. You've saved me twice in a week." Miranda rubbed her head again. "I've also bumped my head twice in a week."

Alex sat up, pulling her with him. He took her hands, turned them over, and examined her palms.

"These cuts need to be cleaned," he said. He helped her to her feet. "Let's go back to the house and take care of them. We'll check out the view later."

They made their way back to the house, avoiding the group on the patio by going in a side door. Alex led Miranda upstairs to the bathroom.

He turned on the water, grabbed the soap, and washed her hands, being careful not to hurt her. Once he finished cleaning her cuts, he pulled her into the bedroom near the bathroom. He ordered her to sit on the bed so he could examine her head, then he kneeled in front of her, holding her hand as he checked the slight bump under the hairline on her temple. Alex brushed his thumb over it and stopped when she winced.

"Ouch."

"Sorry," Alex whispered. "Do you want me to get you an icepack?"

Miranda shook her head. "I'll be okay." She smiled at him. "You're a good man, Alex Peters."

"I am?"

She nodded. "Yeah, the best. It scares me."

"Scares you?" He sat back on his haunches. "I don't understand."

"You're too good to be true."

"Is that a bad thing?"

Miranda shrugged. "I'm not sure I'm good enough for you."

Alex wondered if she ever thought she was good enough. They never talked about her and her relationships. He knew what the press and the tabloids said, but after they destroyed Chris and Sofia, he was hard-pressed to believe much of what they said. He'd seen enough people hurt in Hollywood by the gossip rags and paparazzi.

"You're ridiculous, Miranda."

"I'm not, though." She looked at him through half-closed eyes, her lashes shadows on her cheeks. "I'm a spoiled, snotty diva. Ask anyone. Nobody wants a diva like me. I haven't had a serious relationship in years. I have three friends—one of them is my brother and the other two work for me. I'm a terrible person. Is it any wonder someone wants me dead?"

Alex stared into her eyes. He'd worked with enough actors over the years to see the truth and know when they were putting on a facade. Miranda hid behind the spoiled, snotty diva persona. She used it as a shield.

"That's not who you are. Maybe if you let people in…"

"Why should I?" she blurted. "Nobody wants to know the real me. It's easier to let them think the worst. Then I won't get hurt."

Alex closed his eyes and dragged in a deep breath. He exhaled slowly before he spoke. "I won't hurt you."

"But you won't tell me what's bothering you, why a relationship with me seems so scary. I want to believe you won't hurt me, but I can't stand the uncertainty and the indecision. I like you, Alex. It's crazy. It's been four days, but there's this insane pull when we're together. I'm willing to see where it goes. I *want* to see where it goes, but only if you do too."

Alex nodded. The insane pull was there for him too. He almost let it slip away because he was too busy trying to figure out his feelings and their deeper meaning.

"I also want you to kiss me again," Miranda whispered.

Alex smirked and chuckled under his breath. "Is that what you want?"

She nodded. "Yes, please."

Alex wrapped his arms around her and kissed her—a desperate, needy kiss that shifted his entire world. He pushed her back onto the bed, drowning in the sensation of having her beneath him, of kissing her and tasting her. She made little gasping noises in the back of her throat. The sound drove him wild with need, though he hardly heard her over the roar of blood in his ears when his lips traveled to her neck. She moaned his name, and his cock jumped.

He wanted more.

Chapter Eighteen

MIRANDA

Miranda wrapped her hands around the back of Alex's neck, dug her fingers in his hair, and held him to her as the kiss deepened. Alex rolled to his side, keeping his arms around her as one hand slid up her back and into her hair, twisting the strands around his fingers. They lost themselves in the overwhelming sensations of kissing and being together.

She fumbled with the buttons on his shirt until he pushed her hands away and pulled it off, then she slid her hands under his t-shirt, cold fingers against his hot skin. Alex drew her leg over his hip, his fingers digging into the soft flesh of her thigh and ass, and tugged her tight against him. He swallowed her moans as their bodies rocked together.

Miranda pulled his hair as he sealed his lips over her pulse point and sucked, the breath tearing in and out of her. Every atom in her body pulsed and buzzed with an intense need she never knew existed.

Alex eased his hand under her shirt and dragged his strong fingers over her ribs and belly, leaving a trail of goosebumps. She shuddered, a huffing giggle bursting out of her.

"Tickles," she rasped.

He smiled against her ear. "Maybe I shouldn't be so gentle."

Lust, raw and primal, skittered along her spine at the weight of his words. "Maybe you shouldn't," she challenged.

Alex growled and flipped Miranda to her back, his weight settling over her and pushing her into the mattress. One hand slid up her body and skimmed her breast before settling around her throat and squeezing a little as his mouth covered hers. She wrapped both of her legs around him, pulling him into her as her body lit up with need and desire.

"Jesus, sweetheart, do you know how much I want you right now?"

"About as much as I want you, you big lug," she gasped. "God, Alex, don't stop." She pulled him back to her lips.

The knock on the door startled them, and for a second, Miranda thought Alex might ignore it. It came again, louder, more insistent. With an irritated huff, he pushed himself off the bed and yanked open the door.

"Hey," Caleb said, "you guys disappeared. Everything okay?"

"Yeah, we're fine," Alex responded.

"Chris is looking for you. Something about grilling steaks?"

"We'll be right there."

Caleb chuckled. "I can tell him to wait—"

"Thanks, but we'll be down in a minute." Alex slammed the door in his brother's face and turned back to Miranda with a sheepish grin. "I guess we better go."

Miranda pushed herself to her knees and gestured for Alex to come closer. He stepped into her personal space with a grin on his face, his hand falling to her waist.

"Yes, ma'am?" he asked.

She caught his lips with hers, loving the low rumble emanating from his chest. The kiss was over far too soon.

———

Miranda didn't get Alex alone again until after the wedding, though not for lack of trying. They weren't sleeping in the same room—a request from Alex. Instead, Alex's room was upstairs and hers was in the basement next to Sofia's best friend. There was always something to do: a meal to eat, people to meet, decorations to hang, or even obnoxious paparazzi to remove—a job Alex happily took on himself.

Friday night, she dragged herself to bed around one a.m. while Alex stayed up to help put the finishing touches on the decorations. She was asleep before her head hit the pillow.

Saturday, the day of the wedding, she tried cornering him, but Seth, Caleb, or Chris always appeared and spirited him away for another task. Eventually, she gave up chasing Alex around and decided to enjoy herself.

The wedding was beautiful. Chris and Sofia were an amazing couple and obviously deeply in love. Pretending to be Alex's girlfriend was fun; he was different when he was off duty. He was easy to get along with and very different around his friends and family. She liked this Alex a lot. Miranda enjoyed herself for the first time in forever. She drank, laughed, and danced with Alex, Caleb, and even Chris' best friend, Seth.

She enjoyed herself so much she had no idea how much time passed until Alex plucked her out of Caleb's arms and led her to a seat along the wall. She winced and kicked off her shoes.

"Are you having fun?" Alex asked.

"I am. What time is it?"

"Midnight," he said. "You've been dancing the night away."

"Yeah, well, I'm paying for it. My feet are killing me."

Alex slid his hand over her bare leg, took hold of her ankle, and pulled her foot into his lap. He pressed his thumb into her instep and rubbed gentle but firm circles.

She hummed. "Oh my god, that feels good." She rested her head against the back of the chair, bit her lip, and held back a groan as her eyes drifted shut.

"Why don't we call it a night?" Alex whispered. "Let's go back to my room and talk."

Miranda opened her eyes, a giggle sneaking past her lips. "Is that what you want to do? Talk?"

Alex laughed and shook his head. "Among other things. I believe there is a raincheck to be collected. And we really should talk."

"Let's start with why you stuck me in the basement," she teased.

"Sorry. I only said we weren't in the sharing-a-room stage yet. Sofia decided to put you in the basement."

"I like Sofia, so I'll forgive her. You, on the other hand—"

Alex snorted. "You're funny. Come on. Let's go talk."

"Yes, sir," she quipped.

Alex picked up her shoes and took her hand. She followed him back into the house, murmuring good night to his friends. Her heart fluttered in her chest and her hands shook; it was like she was a teenager again. Her head spun with the implications of what was going to happen.

Alex led her through the house and upstairs, stopping outside his bedroom door. "You want to come in?"

"I'm standing here, aren't I?" she asked with a laugh.

Alex's eyebrow shot up and he tipped his head to one side. "How much have you had to drink?"

Miranda held up her finger. "One glass of champagne. I'm not drunk if that's what you're asking. I have all my faculties about me." She eased closer and placed her finger on his chest, tracing the lapel of his suit jacket. "I know what I'm doing and what I want."

"Oh? What's that?" he asked.

"You." She pushed up on her toes and kissed the corner of his mouth.

Alex opened the door, ushered her inside, and turned the lock behind her. He slipped off his jacket and tie, then undid the top two buttons of his dress shirt. He sat on the edge of the bed and looked at her.

Miranda pushed a hand through her hair, pulling the pins free, letting it fall loose around her shoulders. She took a deep breath before stepping between his legs, cupping his face in her hands, and tipping his head back to look into his eyes.

"I don't know what this is, Alex," she said. "I don't know what you're doing to me. It scares me."

"It scares me too. You're my client—"

Miranda cut him off with her mouth on his. They broke apart, and she rubbed her thumb along the edge of his jaw, her nose bumping into his.

"Tonight, I'm not," she whispered. She reached back and unzipped her dress, letting it fall to the floor and pool at her feet. She was vulnerable, embarrassed, crazy, irrational, and out of her mind, but she wanted this. Wanted him.

Alex rose to his feet, took her in his arms, and kissed her. He ran his hands up and down her body, his touch like fire against her cool skin. He broke away long enough to unbutton his shirt and push off his pants, then she was back in his arms. He laid her on the bed, his lips on her neck as he stretched out beside her.

He kissed her neck, her shoulders, and then his mouth was on her breast, sucking the nipple between his lips. He traced circles along her stomach, over her hip, and into her panties, slipping his hand between her legs. Alex took his time exploring her body.

Miranda sighed and closed her eyes, letting Alex's gentle touch take over her senses—his fingers inside her, his lips devouring her and moving over every inch of skin, licking, nipping, and kissing her as he traveled down her body until his mouth was right over her.

When his tongue touched her for the first time, she couldn't hold back an obscene moan. He suckled the sensitive nub of nerves as he thrust another finger into her, burying them deep inside her. She rocked her hips against his hand and mouth, her inhibitions gone.

Miranda grinded on his fingers, her hands tangled in his hair, holding him against her. She cried out her pleasure and writhed on the bed. Alex groaned, the vibration moving through her, and then she came. Her vision went white, every nerve ending on fire.

Spent and overwhelmed with pleasure, she collapsed against the pillows on the bed. But Alex didn't stop, his fingers still inside of her, twisting and thrusting until she came again. Only then did he pull away, a wicked grin on his face. He kissed his way back up her stomach to her mouth and pressed a kiss to her lips before he sat up and climbed off the bed.

She watched as he moved across the room, muscles flexing, his tattooed skin on full display. She wanted to explore every inch of his body, examine every one of his tattoos, and discover the meaning behind them.

Alex took a condom from his suitcase and removed his boxers, then he was back on the bed, kneeling between her legs and lifting her hips. He pulled her legs around his waist and slid into her, filling her, taking her, and claiming her as his.

Miranda fisted the sheets and threw her head back, holding back her screams of pleasure, mindful of the house full of people. Alex balanced above her, his eyes locked on hers as he pumped his hips.

"God, sweetheart, you're amazing," Alex rasped, thrusting harder. He slid his hands under her, guiding and encouraging her to move with him. He gripped her thigh tight, his fingers digging into the flesh. A grunt left him as he sank deeper into her.

Her hips snapped up to meet his, her hands around the back of his neck, dragging him back to her mouth.

Alex set a manic pace, driving into her hard and erratic, burying himself deep inside her. Miranda met him thrust for thrust, clawing at him and holding him tight against her, every move pushing her back to the edge of intense pleasure.

He grabbed her hair and tugged her head back as he returned her kisses. She wrapped her legs around his waist, urging him to move, pulling him into her. She hit her peak and fell, another orgasm taking her. Several hard thrusts later, Alex was right behind her, his body tensing, grunting as he came.

Alex kissed her, nipping at her lower lip and licking over it to ease the hint of pain. He collapsed, sprawling over her. He took her hand, pulled it to his mouth, and kissed the back of it.

Miranda ran her fingers through his hair, basking in the pleasure pulsing through her body.

"Wow," she said. "That was crazy good."

Alex propped himself on his elbows and grinned at her. "Crazy good? I guess I'll take that as a compliment."

"Mm, it *was* a compliment, gorgeous." She giggled. "It was fantastic."

Alex kissed her, the sweet, lingering kiss making her body sing with renewed need. She wrapped her legs around him, sighing as his weight settled over her and the kiss deepened. He rolled to his side, tucked her against his chest, and sighed heavily.

"What did you want to talk about?" she whispered after a few minutes.

"Hm, later. Too tired."

Miranda smiled, buried her face against his chest, and inhaled his strong, masculine scent. There was no place she'd rather be. She wanted to stay in bed with him forever.

Chapter Nineteen

MIRANDA

"Later" wasn't the next morning or after breakfast. Alex was out of bed before Miranda woke up. Once she realized he wasn't in the room, she dragged herself out of bed, threw on jeans and a sweater, and went looking for him. She found him on the patio, saying goodbye to Chris and Sofia before they took off on their honeymoon.

Once the happy couple was on their way, she and Alex joined the rest of the wedding party for breakfast. Then came an hour of whirlwind packing and loading the car before they said their own goodbyes and left.

Miranda didn't want to go back to L.A.—to the real world. She didn't want to go back to wondering if the person trying to kill her would succeed. She wanted to stay hidden in the mountains, pretending she was Alex's girlfriend. Hell, she wanted *to be* Alex's girlfriend. She was falling hard—harder than she'd ever fallen for anyone before. She liked it.

Miranda turned on her phone twenty minutes outside of L.A. She'd left it off all weekend, and she hadn't missed it. The second she turned the damn thing on, notification after notification appeared. She dropped it in the cup holder next to Alex's. She'd deal with the crap later.

"Everything okay?" Alex asked.

"Yeah. I don't want to think about the real world right now, that's all. I'm having too much fun with you."

Alex snorted. "No one has fun with me. I'm the boring tight ass who doesn't know how to have a good time. Ask anyone."

Miranda laughed and shook her head. "I had fun with you. More fun than I've had in a long time."

Alex chuckled and winked at her. "Fun, huh? You think you might be interested in having fun again?"

Her stupid phone vibrated again, but she couldn't take her eyes off of Alex. She snatched it from the cup holder and tore her eyes away from her bodyguard.

[Caleb: Good to see you, bro. I like Miranda. She's great. You should date her for real. It's funny how she looks just like Melissa, though, isn't it? Downright uncanny.]

"Miranda?"

"Hm?"

Alex squeezed her leg. "I asked you if you want to have fun with me again?"

She dropped the phone—Alex's phone—back in the cup holder. "Oh, yeah, fun. Um…"

Alex's phone rang. He answered it.

"Tiny? How are you?"

Miranda picked up her own phone, twisting and turning it in her hands as she leaned against the door and stared out the window, gnawing on her lower lip. Her headache roared back, coming out of nowhere. Except it wasn't the headache that had her holding back tears.

It's funny how she looks just like Melissa, though, isn't it? Downright uncanny.

Melissa. Alex's dead wife. According to Alex's brother, Miranda looked like her. Why hadn't Alex mentioned it? Her stomach twisted in knots, and her heart tried to wrench itself from her chest, a pain like she'd never known burning deep into the core of her being and tearing her to shreds. The Escalade was shrinking, closing in around her, cutting off her ability to breathe.

Alex took the freeway exit leading to her place, driving through the city while talking to Tiny. She watched him out of the corner of her eye, this man who stole her heart in less than a week.

Did Alex have sex with me because I look like Melissa?

Melissa owned his heart; she saw it in his face when he talked about her. She was the love of his life. Miranda was nothing more than a poor substitute for his dead wife. The entire weekend had been a lie. He said he wouldn't hurt her, but he'd done so much worse. He used her.

Miranda couldn't stay locked inside this metal prison, trapped with a man attracted to her because of her resemblance to a dead woman. Alex pulled to a stop at a red light, and she grabbed the door handle, clawed it open, and jumped out. The second her feet hit the ground, she sprinted down the street, ignoring Alex shouting behind her. She shoved her phone in her back pocket, darted down a short alley, hurried across a busy intersection, and ran.

She didn't know where she was going; there was no destination in her mind. The need to get as far from Alex as possible overwhelmed her. She ran until her sides ached, her calves burned, and her lungs felt like exploding.

When she stopped, she was in a residential neighborhood with modest homes. Ignoring the ringing cell phone in her pocket, she wandered the streets until she found a small park with a smattering of playground equipment and several benches set back from the street. Exhausted, she dropped onto the nearest bench and cradled her head in her hands, the breath tearing in and out of her throat as the blood pounded in her ears.

What am I doing?

She was running away. Again. Any time things got crazy or difficult in her life or didn't go her way, she ran away. It was her modus operandi. Every gossip website and hate monger on social media liked to remind the world she couldn't face her problems head on. Instead, she hid from them, hoping they would go away on their own.

Unfortunately, they were right.

When she broke up with her college boyfriend, she hid in her room for two months; when she lost a coveted role in an Abrams film, she'd gone to a mountainside retreat for six weeks and refused to audition for another eight; and when she'd lost the Golden Globes, she'd hid out at her grandparents for a month.

It's what I do.

True to form, she'd done it again. Instead of talking to Alex and getting to the bottom of what the hell was going on, she ran. Literally. Once again, the haters were right.

Miranda had hoped things between her and Alex were becoming serious. But if Alex's feelings weren't genuine, it wasn't possible. If his attraction to her was because of her resemblance to the woman he *actually* loved, she would never know how he really felt about her. Not as long as the ghost of his wife stood between them. Her stomach hardened into a tight knot that rotted her from the inside out, and tears filled her eyes.

Her phone rang again. She took it out of her back pocket and stared at the screen until it stopped. Fifteen missed calls from Alex. Her finger hovered over his name, but she couldn't bring herself to call him. It rang again. She sighed and hit the answer button.

"H-hello?" she stammered.

"Where are you?" Alex shouted.

"I…don't know."

"Miranda." His cold, angry voice sent a chill down her spine.

She swallowed around the lump in her throat and looked around, trying to get her bearings. She spotted a street sign on the corner and gave Alex the names.

"Stay there. I'm coming to get you," he ordered. His voice softened. "Are you okay?"

"Yeah. I'm sorry."

"What were you thinking?"

"I wasn't." She cleared her throat. "I am sorry I ran. But I think there's a lot we need to talk about."

Chapter Twenty

ALEX

Miranda's words echoed in his brain.
There's a lot we need to talk about.

The understatement of the century. If they put aside everything else—her being his client and him dealing with the untimely death of his wife—there was still the not-so-minor issue of her resemblance to Melissa. No wonder his head was all kinds of screwed up.

Alex felt something for Miranda. Hell, he'd slept with the woman. It was more than sex, though. He wondered if his feelings were genuine or if it was because she looked like Melissa, the only woman he ever loved. His attraction to Miranda was real, but so was the overwhelming guilt he suffered.

He couldn't just forget her. His love for her had been too pure, too real and consuming. He feared getting involved with a woman who looked like Melissa would tarnish his memories of her and what he felt for Miranda.

Last night with Miranda was phenomenal, an incredible release. Unfortunately, it only increased his confusion and made him doubt his true feelings. Worry and regret plagued him.

It took him less than ten minutes to find Miranda. He parked on the street next to the small playground in the residential neighborhood and saw her sitting on a bench under a large tree. He watched her for a minute before climbing out of the SUV and closing the door.

God, she's beautiful.

Her eyes met his as he crossed the green grass to stand in front of her. She rose to her feet and rocked nervously on her toes.

"I'm sorry," she mumbled.

"Let's go back to the mansion," he said, taking her elbow and leading her back to the SUV. He needed to get her out of the open. "We can talk there." He opened the passenger side door and ushered her inside.

The silence in the car was thick and awkward. He knew Miranda had seen the text from Caleb; he blamed himself for that. He should have told Miranda she looked like Melissa and made it clear why his attraction to her confused and confounded him. Instead, he let it go too far.

Alex breathed a sigh of relief when they pulled into the mansion's driveway. He parked on the side of the house and cut the engine. He opened his mouth to say something to Miranda, though he wasn't sure what, but Tiny emerged from the kitchen door, Tara beside him. Angela stood at the top of the steps, arms crossed and eyes narrowed. As usual, Alex didn't know what she was thinking. He reached for Miranda, but she pushed open the door and stepped out of the car. He quickly followed.

"Hey, boss," Tiny said. "Everything okay? I expected you forty-five minutes ago."

Tara headed straight for her friend, greeting her as she stepped from the vehicle. She whispered to Miranda, asking her if she was alright, but Miranda brushed it off, muttering something about a headache.

"Traffic," he lied, turning his attention back to his partner. "Anything to report?"

Tiny shook his head. "Not yet. I put feelers out on Brady Gaither like you asked, but I have heard nothing."

"Let me know when you do," Alex said.

He patted Tiny on the shoulder then followed Miranda and her entourage. She went straight to the kitchen cabinet, grabbed a bottle of aspirin, and a glass of water. She took the pills and downed the water, then leaned against the counter, her eyes closed and her face pinched in pain.

"Can I get you anything?" Tara asked.

Miranda shook her head. "No. I'm gonna lie down for a while."

"We need to talk about your schedule for the next couple of days," Angela said. "You played hooky for the last three days, neglecting your responsibilities. We don't have time for you to take a nap."

"Too bad," Miranda snapped. Without another word, she left the kitchen and headed for the stairs.

Alex followed her but paused at the bottom of the stairs, wondering if she wanted him to go with her. His answer came a few seconds later when she turned back and gestured for him to join her.

In her room, Miranda kicked off her shoes and climbed onto the bed. She laid on her side, her pillow tucked under head and her eyes on him.

"Do I really look like her?" she asked. "Like Melissa?"

Alex sat on the edge of the bed, head down, hands folded between his knees. "Yeah, you do." He sighed. "People told me you did, but I brushed it off. I didn't realize how much the two of you looked alike until last week when you opened your front door."

Miranda sat up and pushed a hand through her hair. "Is that why you kissed me? Why you're attracted to me? Because I remind you of her?"

There it was, the question Alex had been dreading. He hoped being honest with her would be enough.

"No, that is not why I kissed you—"

"Really, Alex?" She was obviously skeptical. "I don't believe you."

"Believe what you want," he snapped, "but I'm telling you the truth. I did not kiss you because you remind me of Melissa." Anger pushed the words he'd been trying to form for days from his mouth. "There are similarities between you and Melissa; I won't deny it. Not just looks, but some mannerisms as well. But there are differences too. You're confident where she was awkward, shy where she was outgoing, soft where she was hard, and vice versa. I kissed you because I'm attracted to *you*. I can't stop thinking about you. You,

Miranda. It has nothing to do with who you look like. But I won't lie either. Your resemblance to Melissa is making this crazy hard."

"Alex—"

"Let me finish!" He pushed a hand through his hair and exhaled. "I need you to understand something. I loved Melissa. She was the first woman I ever loved. I don't love easy, Miranda. I never have. Finding Melissa, loving Melissa, meant everything to me. Then I lost her. I wasn't sure I'd ever find another woman who would steal my heart like she did. Then you opened your front door, acted pissed off at me, and turned my world upside down."

"I was pissed at you," Miranda whispered.

Alex laughed, a woeful chuckle even he knew was forced. "You know what else? I'm terrified—terrified I can't protect you and terrified I can't keep you safe from whatever predator has set their sights on you. I didn't protect Melissa when she needed me. I am poison. Melissa's death is proof of that."

"You're not responsible for Melissa's death," Miranda said, shaking her head.

"I keep telling myself that—shit, everyone keeps telling me that—but my heart refuses to believe it." He pushed himself to his feet, unable to sit still anymore. "I'm not even sure I can protect you anymore, not when I feel like this. I should have David bring Will in from Vancouver, have him take over for me."

"I don't want anyone else protecting me. I want you."

Alex shook his head, deflecting her assurances. "I think you'd be better off with someone else. I'm not sure I'm thinking clearly; I'm too emotionally invested."

In a heartbeat, Miranda crossed the room and stood in front of him, her hands on his waist.

"That's why you *can* protect me. That's why I trust you. Because you care. I'm begging you, Alex. Don't leave me. Please?"

Alex pinched the bridge of his nose and sighed. It was unprofessional of him to guard her when his attraction to her blurred the lines. But he couldn't stomach the thought of anyone else keeping her safe; he wasn't sure he trusted anyone else to do it. He wrapped his arms around her and rested his chin on top of her head. "We'll take it one day at a time, okay?"

"You won't leave me or bring in somebody else to be my bodyguard?" she asked. "Promise me you won't."

He sighed. "Alright, I promise." He wasn't sure he was the best choice to protect her, but if she wanted him to stay, then he would.

Miranda rested her head against his chest. "I think this could go somewhere, could mean something. I want to believe your attraction to me is for *me*, not because of my resemblance to someone you once loved."

"I am attracted to *you*," he said. "You."

His mouth closed over hers, and he crushed her to his chest, his hand on the back of her head. His fingers tangled in her hair, desperate to hold her, to keep her close. He wasn't good with words, but dammit, he would make her understand, words or no words.

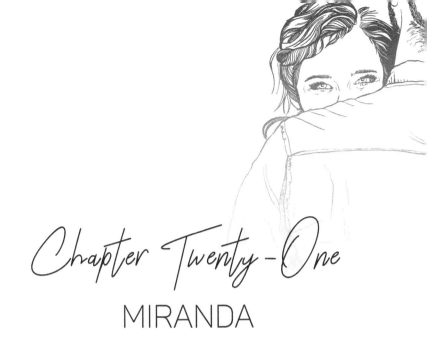

Chapter Twenty-One

MIRANDA

Kissing Alex was intoxicating. She was punch-drunk with lust, want, and need. Every inch of her responded to him. She'd never felt like this before. But knowing Alex had once loved a woman who looked like her made her doubt her feelings. Miranda wanted to believe Alex's feelings for her were real.

Her insecurities overwhelmed her until she couldn't handle it, and she pushed Alex away, her hand to her head. The headache was back, throbbing behind her eyes, making it hard to think.

"What's wrong?" he asked.

"Do you think about Melissa when you kiss me?"

His hand drifted down her arm, drawing goose-bumps to the surface. He took her hand and inter-twined his fingers with hers.

"Come here," he ordered, pulling her after him. He sat on the edge of the bed and guided her onto his lap. "Do you know what I think about when I kiss you? What I feel?"

"No," she whispered. "Tell me."

Alex's eyes locked on hers. "Desire. For you."

Miranda moaned, leaned forward, and pressed a lingering kiss to his lips. Her fingers went to the buttons of his shirt and undid them, her nails grazing his rock-hard chest.

"What else?"

"Need," Alex growled, his hand sliding up her side to her breast. "I need you, Miranda."

She grabbed the hem of her shirt, pulled it over her head, and took off her bra, letting her breasts fall free.

Alex groaned low in the back of his throat, his pupils blown wide, making his blue eyes almost black. He cupped her breast with his free hand, closed his mouth around her nipple and laved it with his tongue as he kneaded it gently.

She reached between their bodies, unbuckled his belt, pulled his pants open, and yanked down the front of his boxers enough to wrap her hand around his hardening length.

"Shit," he moaned and mouthed his way up her chest to her mouth to catch her lips in his. He lifted her, rolled her to her back, sat on his knees between her legs, and hurriedly stripped off his clothes.

His clothes discarded over the side of the bed, Alex pulled Miranda's jeans off before he slipped his fingers into the waistband of her underwear and slowly slid them down her legs, stopping every few inches to press a kiss to her knee, calf, and ankle. He dropped the soft material to the floor, leaned over her, and kissed her.

"I've been wanting to do this all day," Alex purred, his hand between your legs. "God, baby, you're so wet." He brought his hand to his mouth and licked his damp fingers, then he dropped to his knees on the side of the bed, grabbed Miranda's legs, dragged her close, and buried his head between her legs.

Her eyes rolled back in her head, her entire body trembling in anticipation. "Alex, you don't have to," she gasped, shaking her head.

"I want to, doll. I need to taste you again."

A wave of desire washed over her, so strong and overwhelming that she grew lightheaded, dizzy, and unglued. Desire, need, want, and impatience raced through her, setting her on edge.

Alex put his hands on her thighs and pushed her legs open as his tongue darted out and flicked against her. One finger teased her entrance, driving her insane with unbridled bliss.

Miranda's hips bucked, a salacious groan escaping her. She closed her eyes and let herself go to the sensations, her emotions on overload, voicing her pleasure as Alex worked her over. She scrambled for something to hold on to—something to ground her. Her hands landed on the back of his head, and she held him tight against her as he worked to get her off.

It wasn't long before her walls clenched around Alex's fingers, her thighs clamping down on his head. She sucked in short, stuttering breaths, and moaned Alex's name as she came.

He worked her through the orgasm, his fingers digging into her ass as he held her close and moved his head side to side, his beard scratching and burning the inside of her thighs. The intense pleasure overwhelmed her.

"Jesus, Alex," she gasped when she could speak again, "that was unbelievable."

He chuckled, pressed a kiss to her inner thigh, stomach, and breasts before he snatched his pants off the floor and took a condom from his pocket. He rolled it down his length and settled back over her, his hips nestled against hers. His cock brushed against her overheated core. Miranda grabbed the back of his neck and licked at his lips as she took hold of him and guided him to her entrance, one leg hooked around the back of his thigh as he sank into her.

He paused, holding himself still inside her, and stared into her eyes. Overwhelmed by emotions she wasn't expecting, tears sprang to her eyes, and she couldn't breathe until he leaned over and brushed a kiss across her lips.

"It's okay," he whispered. "I've got you." He gripped her hand as he tilted his hips up and into her, burying himself deep inside her.

Alex took his time, his thrusts slow and even, his cock brushing her sweet spot with every pump of his hips. His lips nibbled hers gently, and a groan left him when her mouth opened, and her tongue brushed his. He moved faster, his hips flexing with deep, hard thrusts that had her screaming for more.

Miranda gasped and writhed beneath him as her nails scraped long, red welts into his skin. The orgasm exploded out of her, every nerve, muscle, and inch of her drowning in ecstasy.

Alex held her tight as he thrust one last time. His entire body tensed as he came, his cock pulsing and throbbing as he let go. He rolled to his back, sweat beaded on his forehead and his breath tore in and out of his throat. One hand rested on his chest, his other caught under her.

She flopped over him and placed her head on his chest, needing to feel his heartbeat beneath her cheek. He brushed her hair, a contented hum rumbling through his chest.

After a few minutes, he pushed himself up on one elbow and looked at her. "You look tired. Maybe you should take a nap."

Miranda shook her head. "I'm fine." Except she wasn't. During the incredible sex, she'd forgotten about her aching head, too caught up in the intense feelings she'd been experiencing. But now it was back with a vengeance.

She squinted, watching Alex as he climbed from the bed, muscles flexing. He seemed blurry, far away, and ringed in light. She sat up, and a blinding stab of pain shot through the center of her head.

"Alex?"

"Hm?" He turned back to her, but she couldn't see his face; it was too blurry.

A wave of nausea washed over her. She swallowed back the bile rising in her throat as another stab of pain assaulted her.

"I…I don't feel so good."

Chapter Twenty-Two

ALEX

Miranda had been in the emergency room for five hours, and Alex was losing his mind. It had been hell getting her here; she hadn't wanted to come, insisting nothing was wrong despite the headache, nausea, and blurred vision. Alex forcibly dressed her in a t-shirt and sweatpants, carried her downstairs, and ordered Tiny to take them to the nearest hospital.

Alex worried the head injury at the press junket and the bump from their collision at the wedding did more damage than they realized. Because of Alex's concerns, the hospital staff focused on the head injuries as the cause of Miranda's problems. It took them two hours to eliminate the injuries as the issue.

Once they realized it wasn't the head injuries, the doctor sent a nurse to draw blood and run other tests. It left them waiting for answers.

Miranda refused to let anyone else besides Alex into her room, turning away both Angela and Tara. She laid into the nurse for daring to suggest Alex wait in the lobby. He did his best to stay out of the way, pacing on the other side of the room, watching her monitors and feeling helpless. Every fiber of his being screamed at him to fix it, to help her.

"Will you sit down?" Miranda muttered. "You're making me nervous."

He perched on the edge of the chair beside her bed and took her hand. "How's the head?"

"Hurts."

"The pain meds didn't help?"

Miranda shrugged a shoulder. "They made me sleepy. And irritated."

"You should try to sleep," he urged. "It will help with the irritation."

"Ha ha, you're funny," she deadpanned. "What's irritating me is you and your pacing. You're driving me nuts, and you're making yourself crazy. Let the doctors figure it out."

"I hate doctors," he grumbled.

Miranda squeezed his hand. "It'll be fine. Stop worrying."

Alex kissed her forehead. This woman was reassuring him when he should be the one reassuring her. She kept amazing him in ways he didn't expect.

"Ms. Putnam?" A short, bespectacled man in a white coat entered the room, pulling the door closed behind him. "I'm Dr. Goodson. Are you feeling any better?"

"Not really. My head still hurts, and my skin feels like it's on fire."

"Well, I have good news for you. I think we may have figured out what's going on," Dr. Goodson said.

"You did?" Alex interjected. "What is it?" Every scenario imaginable ran through his head, all of them bad.

Dr. Goodson crossed his arms and stared at Alex over the top of his glasses. "I'm sorry. Who are you?"

"A close friend," Miranda said.

"Her bodyguard," Alex said at the same time.

Miranda shot Alex a dirty look. "It's okay, Dr. Goodson. I trust Alex. You can speak freely in front of him."

The doctor flipped through the chart in his hand, his brow furrowed and his lips pursed. He adjusted his glasses before speaking. "Your bloodwork came back. You told Tessa—the nurse—you've been having these headaches for weeks?"

"Yes. They went from bad to terrible about five or six weeks ago."

Dr. Goodson nodded. "Your blood is showing high levels of organophosphate. In laymen's terms, it's an insecticide."

That word got Alex's attention. "Wait? An insecticide? As in a bug killer? Are you sure?"

"I'm positive," Dr. Goodson replied. "I had a patient last week exposed at the plant where he worked. His was an acute exposure. Yours, Ms. Putnam, appears to be a slower, chronic exposure. I suspect you've been ingesting the organophosphate."

"What?" Alex shot to his feet, his hands fisted at his side. Ingesting an insecticide could only mean one thing.

Dr. Goodson nodded and showed the chart to Alex. "Ms. Putnam has been slowly poisoned over the last month or so. It's probably been in her water, coffee, food, or even sprayed over any medication she takes regularly."

"Alex?" Miranda whispered.

He took her icy hand in both of his, his thumb brushing over her knuckles.

"Okay, so what do we do now?" Alex asked.

"The head injury you sustained earlier in the week may have saved your life," Goodson said. "The insecticide caused the headaches you've been experiencing. It would have gone undetected if you hadn't hit your head. Fortunately, we caught it early enough to treat it. We are going to give you atropine and pralidoxime to counteract the effects of the organophosphate. You should be able to go home in a few hours." He tucked the chart under his arm. "Let me know if you need anything."

Alex shifted into work mode as soon as the doctor stepped out of the room. He pulled his cell phone from his pocket and called David.

"Alex? What's up?"

"I need a full team at Miranda's ASAP," he said by way of greeting. "Double the people patrolling the house. Put anyone available on her place. I need someone to come and take samples of everything—food, drinks, medications, and anything she might have ingested in the last month. And I need it done now."

"What the hell happened?"

"We're at the hospital—"

"What did you do now?" David snarled.

"Nothing," Alex snapped. "Miranda wasn't feeling well—nasty headache. I thought maybe it was from the hit to the head earlier this week, so I brought her in. Turns out, the headache—'headaches' since she's been having them for weeks—was because she was poisoned with insecticide. Doctor thinks she's been ingesting it over the last few weeks."

David muttered a few choice expletives. Alex heard papers shuffling amid the curse words flying from his boss's mouth.

"I'll have a team there in an hour," David said. "We'll scour the place, clean it out. Until we find out who's been doing this, we'll bring food in for Ms. Putnam."

"Exactly what I was going to suggest," Alex agreed. "Can you do me a favor and see if you can get Rylan down here from Vancouver? I want him on this. His research skills and intuition about this shit are unmatched."

"Consider it done."

"And try to keep it out of the press. We got out of the house without alerting the damn vultures; let's see if we can continue that. Keeping it quiet might help us ferret out who did this."

"Good idea," his boss said. "I'll check in with you later. I've got some calls to make."

Alex shoved his phone in his pocket. His heart pounded and sweat dripped down his back. He hadn't been this angry in a long time. He was determined to find out who did this to Miranda and would make sure they regretted it for the rest of their lives.

Chapter Twenty-Three

MIRANDA

D r. Goodson wasn't lying; Miranda was home and in her own bed by midnight, curled up beside Alex. He smoothed her hair away from her face as he worked his way through the file on his lap. She was exhausted and nauseous thanks to the medication they pumped into her.

When Miranda got home, she found people going through her refrigerator, her cabinets, her bathroom, and the guesthouse—every place imaginable. Alex had called David from the hospital, and David sent a team to collect and test everything that might contain the insecticide.

From now on, Miranda could only have bottled water, coffee, or takeout food brought in by Alex or the team from Primetime Security. In short, if Alex or his team didn't bring it to her, she couldn't have it.

She went from one bodyguard and a driver to a group of bodyguards—Donald, Jill, Stan, and Tiny. Someone named Rylan who Alex claimed to trust with his life, though he wouldn't say why, was on his way from Vancouver at Alex's request.

"What are you reading?" she asked.

Alex closed the file and set it on the bedside table. "I was going over your public appearances for the next few days. I think we should cancel—"

"I can't cancel anything," she interrupted. "You know that. I'm the leading lady in the damn movie, and the ribbon cutting for the soccer center is tomorrow. The studio execs will go ballistic if I skip the premiere, and I cannot miss the ribbon cutting."

"Maybe Cooper can handle it alone," Alex suggested.

"It's the *Putnam* Youth Soccer Center," Miranda reminded him. "We both need to be there."

"Look, I can get on board with the movie premiere. It's three days away. I don't like it, but I'll agree to it. It might give us time to figure out who is behind this. But the ribbon cutting ceremony? Tomorrow? It's too soon."

"Alex, whoever is behind the attempt on my life thinks we're still clueless about the insecticide, right? Only you, me, the people from Primetime, and my brother know about it. That's it. No one else." Miranda pushed herself upright and leaned against the pillows behind her. "I think it's okay. I have to go. I *have* to, Alex."

Alex huffed loudly and crossed his arms over his chest. Miranda disliked the look on his face, but she wasn't backing down. She crossed her arms as well and stared at him.

"Okay," he sighed. "But…"

"Of course, there's a but," she mumbled.

"It needs to be a brief appearance," he continued. "The entire security team will attend, and we will check the center beforehand for any potential security issues. You can make a brief speech, cut the ribbon, and then we get out. No press afterward, no hanging around for photo ops. In and out. Understood?"

"Understood. I'll talk to Cooper. He can do the press and photo ops. He's the soccer superstar; they'll want him anyway. The questions they ask me will be about the threats to my life. I don't want the focus on me; I want it on the center."

"Thank you. I thought that would be harder."

Miranda lay down and took his hand, holding it tight. "I won't argue. You want the truth? I'm absolutely terrified. Before, it was empty threats. But after everything that's happened—the shooting, the texts, the note, and now the poisoning—how could I ignore it? There is someone out there who hates me enough to want me dead."

Alex stretched out, pulled her into his arms, and pressed his lips to her temple. "I'm sorry you're going through this," he whispered.

Miranda wrapped her arms around his waist and snuggled close. Being in his arms helped her forget her problems. The rhythmic beat of his heart was a deeper comfort than she'd ever known existed—a comfort she didn't know she needed until he came into her life.

"Don't you get tired of sleeping in your clothes?" she mumbled.

"Sometimes." Alex chuckled. "Go to sleep."

"You'll figure this out, right? Who tried to kill me, I mean?"

"If it's the last thing I do," he promised.

Angela pounced on Miranda before she even got downstairs, cornering her in her bedroom.

"What the hell is going on?" Angela demanded. "Why is this place crawling with security?"

Miranda pushed a hand through her hair and sat on the edge of her bed. She'd been dreading this all night, explaining what the doctor had discovered. "Alex increased my security, brought in more people. As a precaution."

"Obviously, but why?"

"I ended up in the hospital last night—"

"What?" Angela cut her off, her arms crossed over her chest. "Why didn't someone call me?"

"Because you couldn't have done anything. I'm an adult who doesn't need her manager to hold her hand every time something happens."

Angela rolled her eyes. "I could have controlled the press."

"There was no press," Miranda snapped. "They don't even know I left the house. Alex was very discreet."

"It's gonna get out. They'll want to know why you were there and what happened. I need to get in front of this. I'll make some calls." She turned to go.

"Wait, a minute!" Miranda shouted, stopping her. "Who are you calling?"

"My contacts within the press." Angela shrugged and turned to go again. "I'll put out an official statement."

"No."

"No?" Angela stopped at the door, her hand on the knob. "What do you mean, no?"

"Why tell the press? They don't know anything, and I don't think we should be the ones to tell them."

"We need to squash any rumors," her manager explained in a clipped tone. "If I release a statement, blame it on exhaustion or something, you should be okay. Maybe it won't sink you. You haven't looked so great in the press lately."

"I don't want to release a statement unless we absolutely have to. Alex said he wants to keep it out of the press too."

"I don't give a shit what Alex said—"

"Well, I do," Miranda said, rising to her feet. "The last time I checked, this was *my* life. No statements to the press. Period."

"You know this thing with Alex is bullshit, right?" Angela snapped.

"What the hell are you talking about?"

"You and your bodyguard. You're fucking him, aren't you, Miranda?" Her eyes narrowed, and a nasty smirk danced across her lips. "The only reason he's sleeping with you is because you remind him of his wife. Once this job is over, he'll go on his way, telling everyone how he bagged the pretty actress that looks like his dead wife, and you'll be left alone."

Miranda gritted her teeth and pointed at the door. "I think you should go, Angela. Take a couple days off. I'll see you at the premiere."

"Miranda—"

"Take the time off, Angie. It's either that, or I fucking fire you for being a bitch. Go."

Angela huffed, yanked open the door, and stomped down the hall. Miranda followed her, worried she would say something to Alex. Angela snapped at several people on her way downstairs, and a few seconds later, the front door slammed so hard it reverberated through the front foyer.

Miranda sank to the stairs and watched the strangers taking over her house. She was living in one of her movies. Someone was trying to kill her, she'd fallen for her bodyguard, and she'd just had the climactic fight with her manager. What else could go wrong?

"Hey, you okay?" Alex sat beside her, his arm snaking around her waist.

"I guess." She sighed and rested her head on his shoulder. "I pissed off Angela."

"Why?"

"I told her not to contact the press. She said she wanted to 'get in front of it,' but I said no."

"Get in front of what? The poisoning?"

"I don't know. I didn't get a chance to tell her about the poisoning. I said I was in the hospital and then she started talking about releasing a statement. I don't even know what she wanted to say. I just told her no. Then we argued about you."

Alex snorted. "Dare I ask why?"

"It's not important." Miranda shrugged. She wasn't interested in telling Alex what her manager said. It would only increase the tension. "I gave her a couple days off to cool down. Let's forget about it, okay?"

Alex nodded and kissed her temple. "Come on. I'll introduce you to my brother."

Miranda furrowed her brow. "Your brother? Caleb? I already know him."

"Nope, not Caleb. Rylan. He got here a few minutes ago. He's helping with security." He stood up, pulling her with him. "You're gonna love him. Everybody does."

Chapter Twenty-Four

ALEX

"Miranda, this is my little brother," Alex said. "Rylan, this is Miranda."

Rylan smiled and shook Miranda's hand. "Nice to meet you."

Miranda giggled. "Wow, *three* attractive brothers in one family. Great genes."

"Aw, so you know Caleb too," Rylan said and chuckled, his grin widening.

"We worked together once," she explained. "I do *not* remember you and Alex hanging around, though. I think I would have noticed you two."

"It was probably before he got all famous and stuff." Rylan snorted. "Anyway, how are you feeling?"

"Okay, considering everything. I could use a cup of coffee and some food."

"Well, as usual, I'm here to save the day." Rylan pointed at the table behind him where he'd put a box of donuts and to-go cups of coffee.

"My new favorite Peters brother," Miranda joked, elbowing Alex in the side.

Alex shook his head and watched his brother chat with Miranda as he handed her coffee and a donut. Rylan had always been a charmer, winning over clients with his good looks, warm smile, and easygoing personality. They worked well together, though it had been two years since they were together on a case. David had sent Rylan to Vancouver a few months after Melissa's death to work with a hot celebrity on a long-running television show. Since then, he'd only been back for a day or two, here and there. It was good to have him home.

Miranda laughed again—a sound Alex loved hearing. She'd been understandably quiet since returning from the hospital. Now, she had a smile on her face, and the tension was gone from her back and shoulders.

She and Cooper were due at the youth soccer center in three hours, and Miranda was eager to attend. She'd repeatedly told him it was time to show the world she wasn't the spoiled brat the press painted her to be. Funding the youth soccer center's construction and throwing her support behind it was not only her chance to change people's minds, but it was important to her brother.

Alex disliked the idea of Miranda being out in public, but he understood her need to prove she was more than she appeared to be. The press and not-so-well-meaning fans could destroy someone's repu-tation. He'd seen it firsthand too many times—most recently with Chris and Sofia.

He sent Jill, Donald, and Stan to the soccer center early this morning to scope the place out and work with the local police to secure the event. It helped him feel marginally better. He and Rylan would take Miranda and Cooper over once Alex was confident it was safe and his team gave the okay.

"Enough chit chat, Rylan," he said as he plucked a donut from his brother's hand. "Let's get you up to speed. I'll show you where you can set up."

Miranda excused herself to get ready, leaving Alex alone with Rylan.

His brother followed him to the security office, pulled out a chair, and set to work. He turned on every monitor and opened his laptop. If there was one thing Rylan was good at, it was tech stuff and research. He would be eager to get started.

"How you been?" he asked, sitting down next to his brother.

"Not bad. Thanks for getting me out of Vancouver. I'm glad to be home. I hate playing catch up, though. I feel rushed, like I don't have enough time."

"I thought Tiny filled you in on the way from the airport?"

Rylan nodded. "He did. You know how I am, though. I need to see and experience it for myself. I'll go through the files, build profiles on everyone, and see if I can connect the dots. Are you thinking it's someone Miranda knows?"

"Possibly. It has to be someone with access to the house—maybe the gardener or housekeeper. There is also an assistant, Tara, and Miranda's manager, Angela. Her brother, Cooper, stays here sometimes too. When they hired me, the house was wide open, a lot of people coming and going. I cut it down to essential staff after the note."

"We'll get to the bottom of it," Rylan said.

"Yeah, you better, or David will have my head for demanding I bring you down here." Alex laughed.

Rylan spun in his chair, twisting it side to side, and picked at invisible lint on his pant leg. "You seem like you're doing good. Miranda's nice."

"Spit it out, Rylan." His brother had something to say. One look at Rylan's face gave it away. He took a sip from his coffee cup and waited.

"Are you two…together?"

"Maybe?"

"That's not an answer," Rylan said with a laugh.

Alex rolled his eyes. Damn his always observant brother. "Yes, we are. But you have to keep it quiet. We don't want the press getting wind of it—not while this other shit is going on. Understood?"

Rylan nodded. "Does she know she looks like Melissa?" He spun and stared at his shoes.

"Yeah, she does. Thanks to Caleb. She saw a text on my phone from him."

"Baby brother always was a blabbermouth," Rylan said. "Well, what matters to me is that you're happy."

"Thanks, Rylan."

"Are you?"

"Yes. And I'll be even happier when we figure out who wants her dead."

Rylan turned back to his laptop. "Right, back to work. Tiny said Brady showed his face. When the hell did that happen?"

"A couple time in the last few days," Alex said. "He showed up at Miranda's fundraiser then again at her press conference. He gave me some vague answer when I asked who he worked for, and Tiny still hasn't found out. I can't help but wonder if he's involved in this shit with Miranda."

"Do you know if he has a connection to Miranda?"

Alex shook his head. "No."

"Could he be hanging around her because of you?" Rylan asked.

"I don't know. Maybe. I doubt it."

"That could mean he doesn't have anything to do with this. It could be a coincidence." Rylan tapped his chin, his brow furrowed.

"True. The death threats started before I arrived. To be safe, we need to dig around and see if we can find any connection with Gaither. I want to eliminate him completely. Until then, he's a threat."

"He hates you more than anyone. How did those run-ins go?"

"The first one was okay. He was fake, annoying, overly friendly—typical Gaither shit. The second time, full-on asshole. Crass, humorless, trying to start shit with me in front of Miranda."

"I like her," Rylan said.

"So do I." Alex cleared his throat. "Me and Miranda, we're figuring it out. Or trying to, anyway."

Rylan nodded as Alex spoke, a satisfied smile on his face. "Good. I mean, it's good you guys are figuring it out. Now if we can just—"

"Alex?" Miranda's voice floated in from the hall.

"Speak of the devil," Alex said, pushing to his feet. "Time to go."

Rylan drove the twenty minutes to the soccer center with Alex in the passenger seat and Miranda, Tara, and Cooper in the back. Alex gave everyone a quick rundown on how things would go once they arrived at the Putnam Youth Soccer Center. Miranda and Cooper nodded along as he spoke, but Tara seemed confused at the extra precautions. When he finished, the Putnams huddled together to work on their speeches while Tara took notes on her tablet.

As he drove, Rylan asked more questions so he could get up to speed. One thing Alex always appreciated about his younger brother was his attention to detail.

They parked in the back lot, secured by Primetime personnel before they arrived. Rylan went in first to check with Jill and get a security update. Alex helped Miranda from the car once he got the all-clear from his brother.

CHAPTER TWENTY-FOUR

"I like your brother," Miranda whispered, taking Alex's hand.

"He's a good guy." Alex smiled. "I'm glad he's here." He led her across the lot, held the door for her, and pointed her toward her security team standing at the bottom of the stairs in the lobby. "You nervous?"

She nodded. "Yes. This is important to me. Me and Cooper. I don't want anything to screw it up."

This project encompassed months of work and thousands of dollars to renovate the old building and the grounds into a center for young soccer players. They wanted to help kids who couldn't afford the exorbitant prices charged by club soccer in the area. Cooper worked tirelessly to hire coaches, trainers, and staff; he purchased uniforms, shoes, shin guards, and balls to give the kids a helping hand. Because it was important to Cooper, it was important to her.

"Miranda!"

Miranda turned. Crossing the lobby was Angela.

"What the hell is she doing here?" Miranda muttered.

"Didn't you tell her to take a couple days off?" Alex asked.

She nodded. "Yeah. She shouldn't be here."

Alex stepped in front of Miranda without thinking, shielding her from Angela. The woman stopped in front of him, a scowl on her face.

"You two might want to cool the PDA when you're in public," Angela said, pointing at their clasped hands. "The press is having a field day out there speculating about a relationship between you two."

"It's not anything I haven't been through before," Miranda said. "What are you doing here, Angela? I thought I told you to take a couple days off?"

Angela stood straighter, her shoulders back, and offered Miranda a sickly sweet smile. "I came to apologize. I'm sorry I was difficult." She cleared her throat. "And for the things I said. I brought a peace offering." She held out a to-go coffee cup. "It's from your favorite coffee shop. They made it the way you like it."

Miranda reached for it, but before she could take it, Alex plucked it from Angela's hand. "Sorry. Nothing gets to her unless it's brought in by my team."

Angela rolled her eyes and opened her mouth to protest, but Miranda cleared her throat behind him, and Angela's mouth snapped shut. Alex didn't miss the nasty look she gave him. Two in less than five minutes—he was on a roll.

Tara took the cup from Alex. "I'll drink it. I need the caffeine." She popped off the lid, took a drink, and sighed happily.

The director of the center swooped in to pull Miranda and Cooper away. The ribbon cutting was moments away. The team and Alex split up; he stayed near Miranda while everyone else moved to their assigned positions.

Miranda's speech went off without a hitch, and true to her word, she kept it brief. Cooper said a few words, charming the reporters with his easygoing smile and laid-back attitude. When it came time for questions from the press, they focused on Cooper—the handsome, witty, and budding soccer star—and let Miranda off the hook. Questions directed at her were quickly and effectively turned back to the youth soccer center by her and Cooper.

Miranda was pleased when Alex ushered her and Tara out of the building and into the car, a radiant smile on her face. Cooper stayed behind to answer more questions and hang out with the kids, assuring Miranda he was fine. Alex offered to have Jill stay with him, which seemed to appease Miranda's concerns.

"I am so glad things went smoothly," she said, sighing as she settled into the backseat. She smiled at Alex in the rearview mirror. "I have you guys to thank for that."

"Just doing our job, ma'am." Alex winked at her.

Tara groaned and leaned her head against the window, her hand on her stomach. Her normally bright, friendly face was pinched and red. "Tara? You okay?"

"I'm not feeling very good," she replied. "My heart is racing, my stomach hurts, and I'm nauseous."

"How long have you felt like this?" Rylan asked.

"About an hour, I guess. Ever since I drank that coffee from Angela. Maybe the cream in it was bad or something."

"Anything else bothering you?"

"My toes and fingers are tingling like they're numb or asleep. It feels weird."

"Have you had anything besides the coffee? Any other food or drink?" Rylan asked.

"N…no, I don't think so," she said. "Why?"

Rylan and Alex exchanged a look. Alex's heart thumped wildly in his chest. He took a deep breath and gave Tara a forced smile. "Okay, Tara, we're going to make a slight detour to the hospital to get you checked out."

Miranda grabbed Tara's hand. "Alex?"

"It's just a precaution," he said. "Okay?"

"O-okay. It's not serious, right?"

"I'm sure it's nothing." He prayed Miranda didn't realize he was lying.

Chapter Twenty-Five

MIRANDA

Miranda stared at Alex. "Angela? You think *Angela* did this to Tara?"

"We think she was trying to do it to you," Alex said. "Tara got unlucky."

Miranda rubbed a hand down her face. Her day had gone downhill fast. Her best friend was in the hospital with arsenic poisoning, and Alex thought her manager and *friend*, Angela, was responsible.

"Are you sure? I've known Angela since college."

"How well do you know her?" Alex inquired.

Miranda wanted to punch the concerned look off his attractive face. He had to be wrong. *I don't believe it.* She closed her eyes and took a deep breath. Angela was her friend, her manager, and one of the few people who stuck by her through the years. Angela would never hurt her.

"What kind of question is that?" Miranda snapped. "I *know* her. She's my friend."

Alex crossed his arms over his massive chest. "Did you know her roommate sophomore year of college died?" He didn't wait for Miranda to answer. "She was poisoned. The police questioned Angela, but they didn't have enough evidence to hold her. And in high school, the police accused Angela of stalking a girl, messing with her, and almost keeping her from graduating because of some boy. Were you aware of this?"

Miranda flinched and shook her head. It was a surprise to her. She thought she knew everything about Angela. But even with this new knowledge, she was compelled to defend her friend.

"I don't believe it. That doesn't sound like Angela."

"Rylan looked into her background. They didn't formally charge her with anything, but it wasn't hard to find the information. He made a few phone calls and dug it up. Trust me, Miranda—it's true."

Miranda dropped to the couch, her head in her hands. "But why? Why does she want to hurt me? There must be some mistake. Maybe it wasn't the coffee..."

"Tiny went back and found the cup Angela tried to give you, the one Tara had this morning. It's with the police now. Preliminary reports show the poison was in the coffee cup."

"You need to talk to Angela. I'm sure she can explain everything."

"We can't find her," Alex said. "No one has seen her since before the ribbon cutting ceremony, not since Tara drank the coffee. She's gone."

"What?"

"She's gone," Alex repeated. "We don't know where she is."

"This is absurd."

"Have you and Angela had any problems? Can you think of anything that might have upset her?" Rylan asked.

Miranda jumped, a breathy squeak leaving her. She'd forgotten he was in the corner. She shrugged. "I mean, there's always something between friends, right?" She wracked her brain, trying to think of something, anything, that might have set Angela off. They always got along well, no contention.

The mermaid movie.

"Shit," she sighed. "The mermaid movie."

"What?" Alex looked confused.

"Five years ago, a year out of college, we were both up for a part in this indie film. I got it. Angela didn't. I knew it upset her, but she said it was what convinced her she should go into management. I hired her as my manager." Miranda pushed her hair out of her face and fell back into the couch cushions. "The mermaid film launched my career. Angela always jokes about it—says if she'd gotten the part instead of me, our roles would be reversed. It gets old after a while."

Alex and Rylan exchanged a look that Miranda didn't like. She heard the words as they came out of her mouth. It sounded like Angela might be responsible for all of this.

"But…but she's my friend," she mumbled again.

How can I believe in our friendship after this?

"It was so long ago." Miranda sighed. "It can't still bother her. She's only joking when she says those things. Right?"

"I'm sorry, sweetheart," Alex said. He pulled a piece of paper from his pocket and handed it to her. "You should probably see this."

Miranda took it and unfolded it gingerly as if it might bite her. It was a list of everything contaminated by the insecticide: water, food, coffee, even the pills she took to help with her headaches. Headaches caused by the insecticide. She tossed the paper on the coffee table and put her head in her hands.

Alex sat beside her and slipped an arm around her waist. Miranda laid her head on his shoulder and closed her eyes. This was insane. Her friend tried to kill her. She was living in a nightmare.

"Let's get you upstairs," Alex whispered. "It's been a long day."

"I'm not tired," she protested.

"Humor me. You need rest."

She followed him upstairs and into her room. The door closed, and she threw herself into his arms, breathing a sigh of relief when he hugged her to his chest. He kissed her forehead and pointed at the bed.

"Get some rest," he ordered. "This morning, you promised me you would take it easy after the ribbon cutting."

"This morning, I didn't know my friend might be trying to kill me." Miranda sighed. She kicked off her shoes and shed her sweater. She threw herself backward on the bed, her arm over her eyes. "I feel like I'm in one of my movies."

Alex sat on the edge of the bed beside her, his hand a comforting weight on her knee. His presence calmed her. Her eyes drifted over the width of his shoulders, the muscles in his back, and over his biceps. His jacket stretched over them, so tight the seams might burst. She wanted to touch them, touch *him*, run her hands over his body, and feel the strength and the power behind them. Miranda pushed to her knees and straddled Alex as her hands curled around the back of his neck, drawing his lips to hers.

The kiss started slowly, though her need for Alex and his for her was a barely restrained passion simmering beneath the surface. Miranda pushed his jacket off his shoulders, her hands running over the arms and shoulders she'd been longing to touch. His hands were on her waist under the edge of her tank top, hot against her bare skin.

"Alex," she whispered. "I need you." She wrapped his blue tie around her hand, pressed her knees into the mattress, and pushed herself closer to him.

A low growl erupted from his chest as he pulled her shirt over her head and dropped it to the floor. Alex kissed up the line of her throat, across her shoulders, and back to her neck. He traveled to the bottom of her jaw then moved to her mouth, nipping at her lower lip until she opened to him. His hands slid up her back and beneath the straps of her bra, pulling them down her shoulders and freeing her breasts. He cupped them, his fingers circling the nipples, bringing them to attention.

Alex tucked his hands under Miranda's ass, lifted her, and rolled her onto her back. He leaned over her, one knee between her legs, pressing against her. Heat flooded her. He took her breast in his mouth, and his tongue gently swirled the nipple, teasing her until her back arched and one hand fisted in the comforter beneath her, the other holding Alex's head to her breast.

They removed their remaining clothes, taking their time to explore each other. Miranda wanted to memorize every inch of him—every scar, mark, freckle, tattoo, everything.

Alex did the same with her, taking his time to kiss every inch of skin as he exposed it, figuring out what made her beg for more and what made her cry out his name in ecstasy.

Miranda burned with need once Alex eased into her slowly, his mouth on hers. Her moans got lost in the heat between them. He pulled her leg around his waist, his hand on her thigh, the other tangled in her hair. His thick cock dragged against her sweet spot with every thrust.

She moved with him, her nails digging into his ass and pulling him into her, wanting every inch of him— deeper, harder, faster.

Alex's control snapped, and his hips flexed as he pounded into her. She wrapped her legs around his waist, her hips rising to meet his. The orgasm built in intensity, pushing at the edges of her control, rising inside her until she couldn't hold back any longer. She let go, coming with a loud cry of Alex's name.

His movements slowed. His deep thrusts made her tingle with orgasmic aftershocks, ending in a deep, possessive *you-belong-to-me* kiss as Alex came, moaning into her mouth.

"Fuck, that was incredible," he groaned, rolling onto his back.

Miranda rolled with him and rested her arms on his chest, her chin on her forearms.

She sighed. "I'm the luckiest woman alive. I'm alive and I've got you."

"Not sure I'm such a magnificent prize." Alex chuckled. "But, yeah, you've got me. Caught me hook, line, and sinker." He kissed the top of her head.

She snuggled closer, laid her cheek on his chest, and closed her eyes. When she was with Alex, she was safe. Protected. No one would dare hurt her with Alex around.

Chapter Twenty-Six

MIRANDA

The morning of the premiere was cold, cloudy, and dreary—odd weather for Los Angeles in June. Miranda wondered if she should rethink her wardrobe choice for the evening; maybe a sleeveless gown wasn't a great idea. She stared at the line of gowns hanging in the hotel room while she sipped the coffee Alex brought her.

Angela was still missing. Miranda didn't know if she should be grateful or worried. The more Alex and Rylan dug up on her so-called friend, the more frightening things got. Angela was truly out of her mind.

According to Alex, Stan and Jill paid an informal visit to Angela's apartment. They found several pre-paid cell phones, along with open bottles of insecticide and rat poison in a hall closet. They also found two notes written in a similar style to the ones Miranda received.

Rylan ran a thorough background check, digging into Angela's past. He uncovered information about Angela's questioning regarding her roommate's death. She had, in fact, been the prime suspect. But the police couldn't prove she was involved. Rylan also found two restraining orders. One was from an actress Angela had sworn "begged me to be her manager," but the woman claimed Angela stalked her after she rejected her management offer and sabotaged her efforts to hire another manager. The second restraining order was from an ex-boyfriend. Angela drove her car onto his lawn in an attempt to run him down after she'd followed him for days beforehand. Miranda recognized his name; Angela claimed to have dumped him.

It was clear her entire history with her so-called friend was nothing but a lie. Miranda was sick to her stomach thinking about it. Angela had been biding her time, waiting for the perfect opportunity to destroy Miranda. If the studio hadn't insisted on security, Angela might have succeeded.

"Miranda?"

Alex peered around the door. She didn't enjoy the studio's request of having him out in the hall. They wanted her to keep the relationship low key—meaning out of the press. Having him hanging out in her hotel room would raise eyebrows. So he was out in the hallway like a dutiful bodyguard. At least Miranda knew no one would get past him.

She smiled. "Hey."

"Got a minute?" he asked.

"For you, always."

Alex checked the hallway, then he stepped into the room and pushed the door closed. He crossed the enormous room in three long strides, took Miranda in his arms, and kissed her, taking her breath away.

"Mm, wow." She giggled when he released her. "What was that for?"

He shrugged. "I don't like you in here alone. And I don't like being in the hallway."

"I know." Miranda sighed. "It's not for much longer. It's only until we get through this stuff with the premiere, and then I don't give a shit who knows about us. Hell, I'll shout it from the highest rooftop in Los Angeles." She kissed the corner of his mouth and ran her fingers through his hair. "Any word on Angela?"

"Not yet. David had Stan run facial recognition at the airports and bus stations, hoping to catch her leaving town. But so far, there's been nothing. Donald is going to Primetime's office to meet with one of the police detectives investigating Tara's poisoning. David thinks we've got enough evidence to prove she was the one trying to kill you. Don't worry. We'll find her."

Alex's ringing phone interrupted whatever else he might have said. He kept an arm around Miranda's waist as he pulled the phone from his pocket. She rested her head on his chest and wrapped her arms around his waist, her breathing syncing with his. She closed her eyes and let herself forget about everything but Alex. He was her entire world, her everything. She hadn't expected to stumble into something so amazing the day she opened her door and found him standing there.

Miranda only half-listened to him, his voice a low rumble in her ear, content to be in his arms, even if only for a few minutes.

"I have to go," Alex blurted, shoving his phone in his pocket. "Jill's downstairs. I'm going to send her up to wait with you."

"Where are you going?"

"Stan found something. Rylan said I need to see it. I promise I'll be back before the red carpet." He kissed Miranda's cheek and disappeared out the door.

"Well, shit," she muttered.

Chapter Twenty-Seven

ALEX

"What am I looking at here, Rylan?" Alex asked. He'd rushed to the office to look at whatever his brother wanted him to see, but so far, it had been nothing more than a video of him frantically searching for Miranda in the crowd of people outside the press junket during the shooting.

"We pulled the video from the surrounding buildings," Rylan explained. "Stan compiled it into one video stream, and we've been going over it." Rylan pointed at the monitor, and his finger hit the center of the screen, earning him a dirty look from Stan. "Watch."

Alex crossed his arms over his chest and watched the screen. Not having any sound was surreal; he remembered everything that happened and every sound—the crowd, the people calling Miranda's name, and the pop of the gun firing. It played in his head as he watched the screen.

He suspected Angela shot at Miranda in another desperate attempt to frighten her. Maybe Rylan had found her in the video. Once they got a hold of the footage, he'd instructed Stan and Rylan to go over it with a fine-tooth comb. If they could find proof of Angela shooting at Miranda, it would make their job easier.

"Is it Angela?" he asked.

"No," Rylan said. He pushed a few buttons on the keyboard and enlarged the picture. "Watch."

Alex huffed and rolled his eyes. He wanted to be anywhere but here, waiting for Angela to cross the screen. He was about to walk away and tell his brother to call him when he had something worthwhile when he saw him.

Brady Gaither appeared on the lower left side of the screen, standing beside the fountain, holding a black object at his side. He raised his hand and fired the gun, smoke flicking from the barrel. He fired six shots total before he disappeared into the crowd.

"What the fuck?" Alex muttered. "Rewind it."

Stan rewound the footage for a few seconds and played it from Gaither raising the gun. He fired, and on the opposite side of the screen, the cement at Miranda's feet exploded. Stan hit a button, and the image froze.

"There's no sign of Angela," Stan said. "It wasn't her shooting at the press junket. It was Gaither."

Alex shook his head. "Bullshit. It had to be her. We found that stuff in her apartment, and the text messages came from her burner phone."

"But we didn't find a gun. I'm not saying Angela wasn't *poisoning* Miranda," Rylan explained. "But Angela didn't shoot at her. We think she took advantage of the shooting and used it as an opportunity to further threaten Miranda. But Gaither took the shot at Miranda."

"I fucking knew he was up to something," Alex growled.

"There's more," Rylan said. "Tiny and I checked into Gaither like you asked, and he's not working for anyone. In fact, he's not working anywhere. There was no reason for him to be at the fundraising dinner or at the press conference. Unless he was there because of Miranda."

"Do you think Angela hired him to scare Miranda?" Stan asked.

"What if it has nothing to do with Miranda?" Rylan said. "I've been thinking about it ever since you told me Brady showed up. What if Gaither shot at *you*, Alex? You know how he feels about you."

Alex closed his eyes and tried to quiet his brain. It was too much to process. He was so worried about protecting Miranda it hadn't occurred to him someone might be after him.

Rylan tapped the screen. "I don't think he was trying to hit Miranda. He aimed for her feet to scare her and prompt you into action."

"It makes sense," Alex said. "He *could* have shot her; he had an unobstructed view of her. One of the bullets grazed me. If Tiny hadn't yelled at me to move, I would have been shot in the shoulder or the back. Or worse."

"Maybe he targeted Miranda because you're protecting her. Trying to make you look bad," Rylan suggested. "If something happens to her, you and Primetime Security will be to blame. There's nothing he wants more than to take the company down."

"So, while we've been focusing on Angela…"

"Brady may have been the problem all along," Ryan finished. "He might go after her tonight at the premiere. She'll be vulnerable. And the studios don't want us on the red carpet. They keep the bodyguards at arm's length. Or more."

"Stan, can you check the guest list for the premiere? And the backstage and press pass list?" Alex asked.

"I have it," Stan said. "The studio sent it over an hour ago. I haven't had time to look at it."

"Check if Gaither's on it," Alex ordered. "Now."

Stan's fingers flew over the keyboard, and within seconds, the list was on his screen with one name highlighted.

Brady Gaither.

"I need to get back to the hotel," Alex growled.

Rylan looked at his watch. "You won't make it in time. Miranda's probably on her way to the premiere."

"Stan, get in touch with Jill or Tiny. Tell them to stall," Alex said. "Tell him to keep her in the car until I get there."

"I'll go with you." Rylan rose to his feet and tucked his gun in his holster. "Keep digging, Stan. I want you to find out what Gaither has been up to since David fired him. And find out where the hell Angela is!"

"Yes, sir," Stan replied and spun around, his phone in one hand, the other typing rapidly on the keyboard. "You'll get it ASAP."

"Let's go," Alex said, pulling open the door and yanking his phone from his pocket. "You drive while I call Miranda."

Every minute away from her was a minute too long. He couldn't protect her if he wasn't with her.

Chapter Twenty-Eight

MIRANDA

Miranda spun in front of the mirror, examining every inch of herself, looking for any flaws the cameras would inevitably find. The dress she chose hugged her curves perfectly and emphasized her hips and breasts, giving her the perfect hourglass figure. It wasn't too short or too long, and it paired well with her incandescent heels. The gold material was decadent, silky to the touch. She wore her hair in a low bun with a few tendrils loose around her face. Her makeup was simple—winged eyeliner, mascara, and a touch of clear gloss on her lips. Her only jewelry was a simple gold ring and small hoop earrings.

The sharp, loud knock on the door made her jump. Her stylist laughed, mumbled something about jumpy divas, and yanked open the door. Jill peered around the edge, a scowl on her face.

I wonder if she's capable of smiling.

"You ready?" Jill asked.

"Is Alex back yet? He promised to be back before I left. He's going to drive me."

"No, he's not back. But we have to go." Jill glared at the stylist as the woman pushed past her. They'd gotten off to a rough start; Miranda's stylist didn't appreciate Jill searching her and her things, and Jill was pissed they had forced her to wait in the hall while Miranda had her hair and makeup done.

"Why isn't Alex coming back?" Miranda asked.

Jill shrugged. "Don't know." She stuck a communication device in her ear, threw the door open, and gestured for Miranda to follow her.

"I'd rather wait for Alex—"

"You don't have time," Jill cut her off. "The studio left strict instructions. We have a timetable we have to follow. Until I hear different, we leave now."

Miranda followed Jill down the hall, irritated with the woman's short, grunted answers. She wanted to know where Alex was and what was taking so long. She wouldn't get anything out of Jill, though. She was too stubborn.

They rode the elevator in silence, both of them staring straight ahead. Tiny and Donald waited outside beside the large black SUV parked at the curb. They met her at the door. Tiny took her elbow, and Donald led the way with Jill trailing behind. Don followed Miranda into the back while Tiny and Jill climbed in front.

Miranda fiddled with the ring on her finger, twisting it as she gnawed on her lower lip. Tiny and Jill were intimidating, and while she was sure they were excellent bodyguards, she didn't feel safe without Alex. Especially after everything that happened. She didn't even want to get out of the car if he wasn't with her.

Her phone rang, the shrill sound startling her. She yanked it from her bag and hit the button with shaking hands.

"Alex? Where are you?"

"Hey, Miranda," Alex breathed. "I'm sorry I'm not there."

She turned toward the window, away from the others, her voice dropping to a whisper. "Why aren't you here?"

"I'm on my way. I swear I will be there as soon as I can. Is there any way you can stall, try to keep from walking the red carpet? At least until I get there?"

"Why? What's going on? Is it Angela?" Miranda asked.

"I'll explain when I get there. But I need you to stall, okay? I need you to wait for me."

"I can try." She sighed. "It won't be easy—"

"Try, okay?" Alex shouted several curse words, and Miranda heard horns honking, tires squealing, and engines revving. "I gotta go, babe, but I'm coming, I swear." The call disconnected.

Tiny caught her eye in the rearview mirror. "Was that Alex?"

She nodded. "He wants me to stall," she explained. "Wait for him."

Jill held up her cell phone. "Stan texted me. He said if we can wait, do it. Otherwise, we stick as close to her as possible."

"Did he say why?" Tiny asked.

Jill said one word. "Gaither."

The SUV slowed to a stop, and Tiny rolled down his window. He conversed with the man at the window, then he inched forward, falling in line behind five similar vehicles.

Miranda stared out the window as the car crept forward, her mind racing as she tried to figure out how she could avoid getting out of the car. She couldn't think of a damn thing. She leaned around the seat as the car stopped again. Her co-star stepped from the dark blue limo in front of them and into the crowd of people, smiling as the cameras flashed.

"Tiny?"

"I know," he snarled, his eyes sweeping the crowd. "I'll figure something out. You sit tight."

"I got this," Jill said. The SUV slowed to a stop, and she jumped out, slamming the door behind her. Miranda watched as she took Gina—the studio head of public relations—aside. Jill gestured toward the car, speaking excitedly. Miranda could only imagine what she was saying.

Tiny checked his phone. "Alex's ETA is six to seven minutes."

Gina shook her head and pushed past Jill despite the angry scowl on the bodyguard's face. Gina grabbed the door and yanked it open.

"Miranda, love," she said was a forced smile, her teeth grinding together, "we don't have time for this. We're on a schedule. Let's go."

Miranda glanced at Tiny out of the corner of her eye. He held up five fingers. *I can handle five minutes.* She squared her shoulders and slid out of the car.

"Sorry, Gina. Momentary panic attack," Miranda said.

Gina smiled, but Miranda knew she was annoyed. Miranda followed the public relations director through the crowd to the end of the red carpet. Her eyes darted around, taking in the people, looking for something, though she didn't know what. Alex had freaked her out.

"Miranda, this is Evelyn," Gina said. "She'll guide you through the press line and keep things moving. All you have to do is answer questions and look beautiful. Easy peasy." When Miranda didn't respond, Gina gave her an irritated look, spun on her heel, and stomped away.

"Ms. Putnam, it's nice to meet you," Evelyn said. "If you'll follow me."

Miranda followed in a daze, her mind on the surrounding crowd, worrying about some unknown threat. Jill and Tiny were right behind her. She resisted the urge to take Tiny's hand.

Evelyn stopped at the end of the red carpet, stepped to the side, and gestured for Miranda to go ahead of her. She looked over her shoulder. No Alex yet.

Miranda forced a smile onto her face and stepped into the spotlight.

Chapter Twenty-Nine

ALEX

"Comms?"

Rylan pointed at the glove box, put the car in park, and caught the box Alex tossed at him. Alex ripped open his own box and fumbled with the tiny earpiece before shoving it in his ear. He cringed as Tiny and Jill's screaming exploded in his head.

"What the fuck?" Alex shoved open the door and hit the ground running. He pushed through the masses of people surrounding the venue. He could only make out the words "Angela" and "knife." It was all he needed to hear.

When Alex rounded the corner, he saw a crowd of people gathered on the red carpet, their attention focused on the center of the rough circle they'd formed. He scanned the crowd, trying to find Tiny, Jill, or Miranda. He edged forward, his hand in his jacket resting on the butt of his gun.

"Alex?" Rylan's voice over the comm broke through the noise. "It's Angela. Stan called, said the studio didn't revoke her pass. They kept her privileges on the red carpet intact."

"She came out of nowhere, Alex," Tiny interjected, his voice unbelievably loud in Alex's ear. "One second, everything was fine, and the next, Angela was on Miranda with a knife at her throat. Me and Jill were watching the crowd. We figured any trouble would come from there, not from behind Miranda."

"Take her out!" Alex ordered.

"We can't get a shot off. She's using Miranda as a shield."

Alex pushed through the crowd, shoving people out of his way, and stepped past Tiny and Jill on the red carpet. Ten feet in front of him was Angela, her arm around Miranda's throat, a knife held below her eye.

"Angela!"

She turned toward him. Her eyes were insanely wide, and a sneer marred her once attractive face. An odd laugh left her, the sound like a strange chorus of out of tune bells.

"There you are, Alex." She cackled. "What took you so long?"

"Hey, Angela, why don't you let Miranda go?" He kept his voice low, calm, and soothing. He wanted to shoot her, but he held out his hands and let her see they were empty. "Let her go, okay?"

"Why? What's the point? We know the outcome, don't we? I know this doesn't end well for me. I'm dead, or I'm going to jail for the rest of my life. Either way, I'm going to go knowing I destroyed Miranda's life."

The knife in Angela's hand twisted and nicked Miranda's cheek. A trickle of blood slid down her face and mingled with her tears.

"You don't want to kill her, Angela," Alex said, inching closer.

"I did," Angela said. "I wanted her dead so bad I could *taste* it. But there's no satisfaction in her death. It would make her a darling to the whole world. But I can make her so ugly no one will want her. No one in Hollywood will ever cast her, and she'll never act again. No one will ever love her again. Especially you. You sure the hell won't want her anymore, not if she doesn't look like your wife."

"Angela, please stop—"

"Stop saying my name!" Angela screamed. She closed her eyes for a second and took a deep breath. "I know it's a negotiation technique. You're stalling, and it will not work."

She slid the knife across Miranda's face under the other cut. Blood rose from the one-inch cut, spilled down her cheek, and crept down her neck. Miranda whimpered and clawed at Angela's arm.

"Alright," Alex said. "Look, there has to be something we can do. Everybody wants something. What do you want?"

"I want Miranda's life to be as miserable as mine," Angela snapped. "After I destroy her looks, maybe she can go and find some spoiled actress to wait on hand and foot. She can spend her life being ordered around by snotty divas. Just like I've spent the last five years of my life being ordered around by her. I'm tired of living in the shadows, tired of being ignored, and tired of watching her live a perfect life while I do the work."

"Angela, I never meant to—" Miranda muttered.

"Shut up!" Angela snarled, cutting off Miranda by jabbing the knife into her cheek and drawing more blood.

Angela was unraveling fast. Out of the corner of his eye, Alex saw Rylan moving to the front of the crowd twenty feet to his right. If he distracted Angela, maybe Rylan could get Miranda away from her. Then no one would have to die today.

Rylan nodded at him, a subtle tip of his head. He knew what Alex was thinking. This would work. It had to work. He took a step forward, while Rylan moved to the right and pulled his gun from the holster.

"Please let her go," Alex said. "Let her go, and we'll talk this out. You, me, and Miranda. We'll figure out how to right the wrongs done to you."

Rylan held his gun against his leg, watching and waiting. Alex took another step forward.

"Alex," Miranda gasped as Angela dug the knife into her jaw.

The gunshots were like two claps of thunder, echoing off the buildings surrounding them. Angela's eyes went wide, and her mouth fell open. She coughed, and blood sprayed from her mouth. Miranda's eyes rolled back in her head as she slumped and slid out of Angela's grip, her weight too much for the now-injured woman to hold.

Alex lunged for Miranda, but the curtain behind her separated and someone jumped out, catching her before she hit the carpet. The same someone who had shot Angela.

Brady Gaither kneeled beside an unconscious Miranda. He wrapped an arm around her shoulder and lifted her, hugging her to his side. In his right hand, he held a gun, smoke rising from the tip. A smirk danced across his lips.

"I can't get over how much she looks like Melissa," Gaither said. "She's only missing a couple of bullet holes." He raised the gun and held it to Miranda's head.

Miranda's eyes fluttered open, and a startled gasp left her when she realized who held her. She struggled to get away, but Gaither gripped her tight.

"What are you doing?" Alex growled.

"Well, I wish I could say I'm protecting her, but that's your job, isn't it?" Gaither chuckled. "Not mine." Gaither trailed the gun across Miranda's cheek, smearing the blood flowing from her cuts. He shook his head and clicked his tongue. "You aren't doing a very good job, are you?"

"Brady—"

"Let me ask you a question," Gaither interrupted. "Why do *you* get everything? Huh? The pretty wife, the great job. A job I had until you fucked it up for me and got me canned. It doesn't seem fair. Why should you get the perfect fucking life? Why should you get everything while I get nothing?"

"I don't have everything," Alex snarled.

"Not anymore, right?" Gaither laughed. "I took care of that."

Bile rose in the back of Alex's throat. Gaither was lying. He had to be. Alex shook his head, refusing to believe the man was responsible for taking his entire world away from him.

"I wasn't trying to hit Melissa," Gaither said and rose to his feet, dragging Miranda with him, his grip on her arm so tight his fingers dug into her skin. He pushed her in front of him.

"I was aiming for the bitchy actress," he continued. "What was her name? Courtney something? I figured if you lost a client, got a client killed, you would lose your job. It would be far worse than anything I had done. If she died, David would have no choice but to fire you. If Melissa hadn't thrown herself in front of Courtney, she'd be alive today. But you trained her too well. Sacrifice yourself for the client, right? She did just what you taught her. Instead of hitting the actress, I shot Melissa."

"You bastard." Alex tensed, set to spring at Gaither, ready to tear his fucking guts out. But he froze when Gaither cocked the gun held to Miranda's temple.

"God, I was pissed. I figured I blew my chance to fuck you over. But sometimes mistakes turn out to be a good thing." Gaither shook his head and laughed. "I guess I didn't realize how much you loved your wife or how much losing her would destroy you. I've never seen you like that. So…wrecked. It was pathetic. I thought I'd gotten what I wanted. Alex Peters side-lined forever. Except you had to come back, didn't you? You couldn't live your life locked in your house, mourning your dead wife. No, you had to come to work, back to your life, and I couldn't accept that. I need you ruined. Like you ruined me."

Miranda choked back a sob, her eyes wide, fright-ened, and locked on Alex's. Gaither pressed the gun against the side of her neck, chuckling when she flinched.

"The shots at the hotel after her press junket? You know that was me, right?" he asked. "I'm sure Stan found me on the surveillance tapes. He was always good at his job."

"Yeah, we saw you," Alex said.

"None of this has a damn thing to do with her." Gaither shook Miranda so hard her jaw snapped shut and her teeth rattled. "I wanted to hit you. I wanted to *kill* you."

"You missed," Alex snarled.

"Oh, I know." Gaither laughed. "And I was pissed. My luck was for shit. Until I saw you with her again. You're so goddamn predictable. Always the protector. I saw it in your eyes at the fundraiser; you would go to any length to protect her. I knew I had another chance to destroy you. I mean, come on? A woman who is the spitting image of your dead wife? I could kill Melissa all over again. Destroy you for good this time."

"What the hell are you talking about?" Alex growled.

"What better way to destroy you than to kill her and make you watch?"

Miranda whimpered and squeezed her eyes closed, her head shaking from side to side.

"Let her go, and I won't kill you." The words were acid dripping from Alex's lips. He was going to tear Gaither's fucking throat out.

"Oh, I'm so scared," Gaither mocked, his voice raised, shrill and annoying. He laughed for the hundredth time.

Rylan moved, catching Gaither's attention. He swung the gun in Rylan's direction, his hand closing around Miranda's throat and squeezing. "Don't you fucking dare, Rylan. I have no beef with you."

"Rylan!" Alex gestured for his brother to retreat, terror roaring through his veins as he watched Miranda gasp for air. Rylan stepped back reluctantly.

"How long, Brady?" Alex asked. "How long has this shit been going on? How long have you been trying to destroy my life?"

"Since about five minutes after you got me fired. I thought I succeeded, too, after Melissa." He brought the gun back to Miranda and shoved it into her ribs. "You keep rising from the ashes. But this time, when I kill another woman you love, I think it will destroy you." He pressed his lips to Miranda's temple. "In fact, I'm sure of it."

A bloodcurdling scream broke through the air, and Jill came flying out of nowhere, slamming into Gaither's left side and knocking him sideways. Miranda wrenched free, dropped to her knees, and crawled toward Alex. Alex rushed forward, leaped over Miranda, and tackled Gaither. The three of them—Jill, Gaither, and himself—fell in a heap. The dark black curtains behind the carpeted walkway toppled over, landing on them.

Alex grabbed Gaither's arm and struggled to get the gun. Jill repeatedly slammed her fist into his kidneys, her legs wrapped around Gaither's, her angry screams deafening. The gun flew from Gaither's hand and landed at Rylan's feet. Gaither shook Jill loose and kicked both feet into her gut, toppling her backward onto her ass. Gaither bounded to his feet, but the curtains on the floor tangled around his feet.

"It's over, Brady," Alex panted, pushing himself to his knees. "Don't do anything stupid."

Gaither snorted. "Oh, I'm way past stupid. I'm not walking away from this." His hand slid into his jacket, closing around God-knew-what. A gun or a knife. Not that it mattered.

Alex's training kicked in. He ripped his gun from his holster and pulled the trigger twice. Gaither stumbled back, but he didn't go down. Grinding his teeth, Alex locked his sights on the center of Gaither's chest and fired.

Chapter Thirty

MIRANDA

The paramedic—Bill, according to his name tag—finished cleaning the cuts on Miranda's face. Only one of them was deep enough to require stitches, which Bill did in a matter of minutes. It stung like a bitch. Fortunately, the painkillers he'd given her dulled the throb.

"You good?" Bill asked. He turned her head to the side and examined the stitches in her cheek. "I don't think you'll have a scar, but see your doctor in the next couple of days." He peeled off his latex gloves and tossed them into a small, blue trash bag hanging behind him.

"Do I need to go to the hospital?" Miranda asked. "Please say no. I am really sick of hospitals."

Bill shook his head. "You can go home. None of your wounds are life threatening. I'm serious, though. Make sure you see a doctor in the next few days."

"I will. I promise."

"She will," Alex said. "You can count on it."

Thank God.

"It took you long enough, Peters," she mumbled.

"The police had a lot of questions," Alex said. He climbed into the ambulance and sat beside her, his hand on the small of her back and his leg pressed against hers.

"I'll give you two a minute alone." Bill patted Miranda's leg, jumped out of the back of the ambulance, and left the door open a couple of inches.

Relieved to be alone with Alex at last, Miranda collapsed in his arms, more tears streaming down her cheeks as she sobbed against his chest. All the pent-up emotions she'd held in burst free, culminating in a desperate, crazy release of tears.

"Hey, it's okay. You're safe," he whispered in her ear. He wrapped his arms around her and pulled her into his lap. "It's over, sweetheart. It's over." He ran his hands over her body, examining her for injuries, even though she was in an ambulance and had been examined by a professional.

"I'm fine, Alex. Bill, the paramedic, said I'm fine."

He smoothed her hair away from her face and kissed her. "I'm only making sure for myself."

"This has been the craziest few weeks of my life." Miranda sighed, burying her face against Alex's neck. "Take me home and help me forget this day."

"Hm, I don't know, Ms. Putnam. I think I'm off duty," Alex teased.

Miranda punched him on the arm. "You're not funny," she muttered.

He grinned. "You love it."

"Yeah, I do," she said, pressing a kiss to the corner of his mouth. "Maybe you too."

"Oh, yeah?" Alex breathed. "You love me, huh? You better be careful or someone from the press will hear you."

"I don't care who hears me," Miranda mumbled, swiping at the tears on her cheeks. "I'll take out an ad in Variety, do an interview on that godawful, shitty Gossip Monger site, whatever. I want to tell the world I'm in love with my bodyguard." She kissed him again. "Take me home, please."

Alex grinned, his nose brushing against her cheek. "Whatever you want, Ms. Putnam."

Chapter Thirty-One

ALEX

The scream tore through him, rattling him to his bones and ripping him from a deep slumber. Alex rolled out of bed, the gun he kept on the bedside table suddenly in his hand. He spun in a circle, pointing the gun around the dark room, searching for something to shoot. He tapped the lamp on the table, and light flooded the room.

Miranda was on the other side of the bed, thrashing and twisting in the sheets, fighting invisible demons, calling Alex's name. He flicked the safety on, dropped the gun back in the drawer, then quickly crawled across the bed to pull her into his arms, his hand on her cheek and his lips pressed to her ear.

"It's okay, baby," he crooned. "I'm right here. Wake up for me."

Her eyes popped open, her shaking hands slowly relaxed their death grip on the sheets, and her feet stopped kicking. He brushed the tears from her cheeks with his thumbs and gently kissed her.

"Alex?" she whispered.

"Yeah, baby, it's me." He pulled the twisted blankets away from her legs and readjusted them.

Miranda threw her arms around him and buried her face in his neck, her hair tickling his nose. Alex held her close in the crook of his arm.

It had been weeks since "the incident" as she called it, and the nightmares were a constant presence. They happened almost every night, tormenting her, robbing her of sleep. Miranda hadn't left the mansion since that night.

Thank God he was a patient man. He promised her every day he would do whatever she wanted to feel safe. If that meant she hid out in the mansion, then so be it. He would hide out with her.

"You okay?" he asked once her breathing slowed and her hands no longer shook.

"Yeah," she sighed. "Sorry."

Alex shook his head. "Don't apologize. Was it Brady or Angela?"

"Angela." She shuddered, and goosebumps rose on her skin under the tips of his fingers. "It's getting better, though, I swear."

But it wasn't, and Alex knew it. Fear was a constant presence in her life—their life. She told him it was better and tried to reassure him, but he knew the truth better than anyone.

"Don't lie to me," he scolded.

Miranda tipped her head back, her eyes glistening with tears, her lower lip caught between her teeth. "I don't want you to worry."

"I worry when you lie. I want to know how you're doing. The truth. I don't want you to tell me what you think I want to hear." Alex kissed her again. "Okay?"

"Okay."

"Promise?" Alex asked.

"Yes, I promise."

He hugged her close and the two of them exchanged kisses, murmuring words shared between lovers, not meant for anyone else's ears. Alex reminded her she was safe, cared for, and loved. He would lay his life on the line for her. Every day. Forever.

Chapter Thirty-Two

MIRANDA

Nine Months Later

Miranda leaned over the sink and stared at the bottle in the cabinet. She scrubbed a hand over her face, hoping—again—the simple gesture would magically wipe away the memories of that horrible day and make her whole again.

The nightmares were a constant presence in her life, coming almost every night. The only thing that helped was knowing Alex would be there to wake her. Her therapist worried she was relying too much on him. Miranda disagreed.

Alex kept her sane. Alex reminded her she had something, *someone*, to live for. If it wasn't for him, she would be dead. If it wasn't for him, she wouldn't be able to even think about her life going back to normal.

Today was the start of her new beginning. Everything was coming full circle, and she was ready to start living her life again. Every day, she woke up and stared in the mirror, praying things would be right with her world.

Today, it has to be. I need to be okay, today of all days.

She snagged the bottle, twisted off the top, and quickly swallowed one of the pills. Once the cabinet was closed, she took a long look in the mirror. She touched up her lipstick and patted a stray hair into place. Miranda smoothed a hand over her simple dress, slipped on the heels she'd chosen, took a deep breath, and opened the bathroom door.

Halfway across the bedroom she shared with Alex, an urge to crawl into bed, pull the covers over her head, and hide away from the world came over her. She closed her eyes and took another deep breath, remembering Alex's promise to keep her safe and protect her forever.

I can do this.

Cooper waited outside the bedroom door. He smiled at his sister, took her hand, and gave it a gentle squeeze before guiding her down the hall to the top of the stairs. Miranda let him lead her through the house, her free hand fisted at her side to keep it from shaking. But there was a slight tremble when Cooper opened the door for her to go ahead of him.

Alex stood on the other side of the room, wearing her favorite blue suit. Miranda focused on him, the fear dissipating as soon as his blue eyes made contact with hers. She slipped her arm through Cooper's and let him lead her across the room. She was afraid she'd have to plaster a fake smile on her face, but seeing Alex and the genuine love in his eyes renewed her strength. Nothing in her life had ever been as real as this moment.

I can do this.

Miranda stopped beside Alex and kissed Cooper on the cheek before taking Alex's hand. A breathy giggle escaped her when he leaned over and pressed a chaste kiss to her lips.

"I think you're supposed to wait until the end to kiss me," she whispered.

"I couldn't help myself." Alex chuckled. "You're beautiful."

The justice of the peace cleared her throat and gestured for Rylan and Tara to join them. Miranda squeezed Alex's hand and glanced back at the small gathering of friends and family there to celebrate the day with them.

For the first time since that day, since "the incident," the fear fell away. Being with Alex forever was right. Perfect.

They could do this.

The End

Author Bio

M imi Francis is a northern girl living in the much warmer southwest with no intention of going back. She's always been a voracious reader, and ever since she was a little girl, stories played in her head, daydreams she turned into intricate stories. It took her more than forty years to put pen to paper and start writing, but she hasn't looked back since. Once her three children grew up and started their own lives, she decided it was time to chase her dreams.

She loves writing contemporary romance because it's fun to write about people letting themselves go and getting down and dirty with someone that makes their blood boil. Mimi stumbled into storytelling by writing fanfiction for her favorite obsessions. People loved her stories, so she grabbed the reins and barreled headlong into writing original fiction.

When she's not busy writing, Mimi loves to binge-watch new shows, fawn over her favorite Supernatural monster hunters, rewatch her collection of Marvel movies, crochet, and spend time with her husband and their dogs.

Mimi wants to give readers an escape and a chance to get away from their everyday lives by being transported into a world of romance with a lot of erotic fun thrown into it, even if just for a little bit.

You can find her at mimifrancis.com or on Instagram and Facebook @author.mimi.francis

Do you want more? Watch for your favorite characters to make an appearance in Seth and Sasha's story, *Private Desires*!